JENKINS, JERRY
Jenkins, Jerry
Stolen secrets
Wheaton, Ill. : Tyndale
House, c2005.
P9-DJU-845
WITHDRAWN

STOLEN SECRETS 2

TYNDALE HOUSE PUBLISHERS, INC., WHEATON, ILLINOIS

RED ROCK MYSTERIES

#1 BEST-SELLING AUTHORS

JERRY B. JENKINS · CHRIS FABRY

Visit Tyndale's exciting Web site for kids at cool2read.com

Also see the Web site for adults at tyndale.com

Designed by Jacqueline L. Noe
Edited by Lorie Popp

Published in association with the literary agency of Alive Communications, Inc., 7680 Goddard Street, Suite 200, Colorado Springs, CO 80920.

Library of Congress Cataloging-in-Publication Data

Jenkins, Jerry B.
Stolen secrets / Jerry B. Jenkins ; Chris Fabry.
p. cm. — (Red Rock mysteries ; 2)
Summary: The quiet community of Red Rock is upset by an apparent abduction attempt on two middle school girls.
ISBN 1-4143-0141-3 (sc)
[1. Truthfulness and falsehood—Fiction. 2. Kidnapping—Fiction. 3. Twins—Fiction. 4. Family life—Fiction. 5. Christian life—Fiction. 6. Mystery and detective stories.] I. Fabry, Chris, 1961– II. Title.
PZ7.J4138Sto 2005
[Fic]—dc22 2004028052

Printed in the United States of America

09 08 07 06 05
9 8 7 6 5 4 3 2

To Bob Neff of Moody Broadcasting.
He blazes trails, inspires vision,
and is a faithful servant.
We are blessed to call him friend.

"ATTICUS was RIGHT. One time he said you never really know a man until you stand in his shoes and walk around in them."

HARPER LEE,
To Kill a Mockingbird

"WE are all in the GUTTER but some of us are looking at the STARS."

OSCAR WILDE

Four words.

That's all it took to turn Ashley and Bryce Timberline's world upside down. Ashley gasped as she stared at her stepfather, Sam. Bryce's jaw fell.

Tears rimmed Sam Timberline's eyes. "I'm so sorry. You have to believe me."

Ashley started to cry. "What are you sorry for?"

"For killing your father."

Kathryn Timberline, the twins' mother, trembled. Leigh, their 16-year-old stepsister, stared at the ceiling. The only sound came from the creaking backyard swing where four-year-old Dylan played.

Bryce finally broke the silence. "How could you have killed him? He died in a plane crash."

Sam nodded, his forehead wrinkling. His hair was only flecked with gray, but he looked like he had aged overnight.

Ashley and Bryce had been so close to him over the past week—the trip to the mountains, a brush with death.

"You killed Dad?" Ashley said, a tear zigzagging down her cheek.

Sam stood and stepped toward them. The phone rang. He hesitated, then walked to the kitchen.

"Mom?" Ashley said.

Her mother simply shook her head.

Bryce gazed out the window at the red rock formation beyond their property line. It stood in a protected county area where he and Ashley liked to drive their four-wheeled ATVs.

Sam spoke quietly into the phone and walked outside. When he returned, he gave his wife a pained look. "I need to leave for a couple of days."

"What?" Bryce said. "You can't just tell us you killed Dad and then leave."

"I want to tell you everything. But I can't. Not now." He knelt before Bryce. "I'm not who you think I am."

"You saved our lives on that mountain," Ashley said.

Sam nodded. "I love you guys. But I have to go."

He went upstairs and returned with an overnight bag and the keys to his new truck. He called Dylan in, gave him a hug, and walked out.

"Leigh?" Bryce said.

She shrugged. "I don't know much more than you."

"Anything is more than we know," Bryce said.

"Everything changed after that crash," she said. "I lost my mom and little sister."

"What do you mean, changed?" Ashley said.

"Where we lived. Even our . . ." Leigh bit her lip. "Look, I don't feel right saying more."

"You're right. It should come from him," their mother said.

"And what about us?" Bryce said, jumping to his feet. "What are we supposed to do? Our stepfather just admitted he's a murderer."

"You're only 13," Leigh said. "I don't think you can handle—"

Bryce gritted his teeth. "You have no idea what I can handle, Leigh." He ran upstairs to his room and stood looking out the window.

"Bryce!" his mother called.

Ashley followed her brother.

"Ashley, wait," Kathryn said. "When Sam can tell you more, he will."

"I thought we weren't supposed to keep secrets," Ashley said from the stairs. "Our whole lives have been a secret. You don't even trust us enough to tell us the truth."

"I don't know the whole truth," her mother said, crying.

Ashley trudged to her room and closed the door. She got out her favorite candle—pumpkin and spice. Then she opened her journal and fell on the bed.

CHAPTER 1

✾ Ashley ✾

I was the first one into the mirrored room at Peak Academy of Dance. We call it PAD. I put my stuff in the corner and started stretching. The last couple of days Mom had spent a lot of time on the phone, I guess with Sam. I had no idea where he had gone. Leigh stayed away from Bryce and me. It was all so mysterious.

Only Dylan was normal. When he gets a scratch anywhere on his body, he puts Band-Aids over it. Today he put three on his right arm, four on his left, one on his forehead, and even one in his hair. It was the first time I'd seen Mom smile in days.

Mom told Bryce that Sam would be back by Saturday, but Bryce didn't seem to care. The two of us hadn't talked much about Sam's confession, but I'd written several pages in my journal.

> *What do you do when you find out your stepdad is the reason you're miserable? What do you do when the man your mother chose to marry says he's responsible for the death of the father you loved?*

Bryce and I had moved to Colorado from Illinois with our mom and little brother. Our real dad had died in a plane crash—the news said it was terrorists, but now . . .

A year later Mom met Sam at a memorial service for the victims. Sam's wife and daughter were killed in the same crash. Mom and Sam fell in love and were married.

Sam adopted us and we took his last name. A year after that, Mom got religious on us. We thought it would pass, but it didn't, and soon Bryce and I both became Christians.

Sometimes when things like this are going on, I walk through life in a daze. Dancing helps me focus. It's kind of like my mom's writing, I guess. I get into another world. The music and the movement take over, and for an hour I go someplace else in my mind.

I didn't want the hour to end. When it did, Mrs. Gunderson came in. She's the head of the academy. She had us all sit down and explained that this would be the last week for candle sales for PAD.

"You know how important this is," she said with a smile, "so I'm expecting big results. And the one who sells the most will win these." She produced a pair of ballet shoes like the professionals wear.

I looked at my own ratty shoes and my heart sank. I had sold only one candle, and that was to Mom. The girls around me squealed and whispered how many each had sold, which made me even more depressed.

While we packed up our stuff, parents peeked in the window, whispering to each other, then escorted their kids outside. Weird. As I walked through the lobby past the front desk, I found the door locked.

"We'd like you to wait inside for your mother, Ashley," Mrs. Gunderson said.

"But I always meet her in the parking lot."

"Tonight's different, dear."

I got a drink of water and noticed one of the dance teachers guarding the back door.

"What's going on?" I said to my friend Hayley.

She shrugged as she changed into her tennis shoes. "Place is on lockdown. Maybe somebody stole something."

"They'd be going through our stuff if that happened," I said. "There's your mom."

Mrs. Henderson rushed in and hugged Hayley, something I had never seen her do. People whispered everywhere, and I was relieved when Mom pulled into the parking lot and hurried in.

"What's wrong?" I said as we headed out.

"Something terrible, Ashley."

CHAPTER 2

Bryce

"*Box out!* Box out!" Coach Baldwin yelled. "Timberline, where are you?"

"Sorry, Coach," I said.

Coach Baldwin tucked the basketball under his left arm and stared at us. Our seventh grade team had finished with six wins and four losses. Now we were playing in a regional league, trying to get ready for the next school season.

"Coronado is probably the best in the league," Coach said. "Let's focus." He called a play and threw the ball to Duncan Swift, our point guard.

I slipped back to my defensive position, and Kael Barnes set a pick on me.

"What's up with you, Bryce?" Kael said, pushing me back and turning. The ball shot past my outstretched arm, right into Kael's hands. He stepped toward the basket and banked the ball in off the backboard.

"That's it! That's it!" Coach said. "Way to push the ball inside." He looked at me. "Move your feet, Timberline."

Later, in the locker room, Kael sat beside me. "You've been spacey all week, Bryce. Boo Heckler after you again?"

I smiled. "Haven't heard from him since he tied my pants in knots." Boo had threatened Ashley and me if we didn't let him ride our ATVs. "Baldwin has him scrubbing toilets during gym class."

"So what's your problem?"

I shrugged. "Nothing, really." No way I could tell him. Ashley and I hadn't even been allowed to tell our friends we had foiled a robbery at Gold Town and had almost gotten killed in the process. I wasn't about to let it slip that Sam said he had killed my real father.

Coach Baldwin said we'd need to wait inside for our parents to pick us up. "And, Timberline, your mom called. Said to leave the ATV and wait for a ride from her."

"What? Why?"

"Your mom must have seen you at practice," Duncan said.

Everybody laughed.

Riding the ATV is one of my favorite things. It's mostly pasture between the practice gym and home. On the dirt road behind the gym I can open the thing up and go fast. I love the sound of the wind on my helmet. With everything going on with Sam, I need all the good things I can find, and the ATV is the best.

I grabbed my backpack and raced down the steps. Mom pulled

up outside with Ashley in front. My sister looked like someone had stolen her tutu.

"Why can't I ride the ATV—?"

"Bryce, please," Mom said. "Get in."

"What's wrong?"

Ashley turned. "Two girls were attacked after school."

"It's all over the news," Mom said. "The report said they were from Red Rock Middle School."

CHAPTER 3

Ashley

I flipped on the radio, hoping Bryce could hear it for himself.

"Again, our top story," the reporter said. "According to police, two middle schoolers in Red Rock were attacked this afternoon and held against their will. Details are sketchy and names have not been released, but the incident occurred shortly after school ended. The girls managed to escape, and police are looking for suspects."

"There's no way I'm letting you drive around with some madman loose," Mom said.

"How am I going to get the ATV home?" Bryce said.

"Sam called. He'll be back tonight. Said he'd pick it up with you."

"What about tomorrow morning? Can we ride them to—?"

"The bus. You're not riding the ATVs until they catch this guy."

I kept an eye on the streets as we rode home, looking for some shadowy figure skulking in the pasture or hiding in culverts. It reminded me of the night in the cabin when we knew someone was watching us, and it turned out to be a gold robber.

As soon as we got home I called Hayley to see if she'd found out anything. She suggested I call Marion Quidley, who basically knows everything. I'm a good student, but Marion makes me look like Goofy with a dunce cap. Marion's had perfect attendance since preschool—not a single sick day—but she can get kind of weird. She has wild theories about stuff like Bigfoot and crop circles. When we went through a drought last year and there were lots of fires, Marion thought aliens were draining reservoirs at night and shooting laser beams at the dry forests, which made me think a day or two out of school might do her some good.

"I haven't heard who it happened to," Marion said. It sounded like she was flipping through some pages. "But there are only so many people who actually walk home from school. I photocopied all the kids' pictures from the yearbook and put an *X* over the ones who take the bus."

"You can't possibly know everyone, Marion."

"No, but I also have the school directory that shows addresses, and I cross-referenced. I've copied the names I don't know."

She read me the list of possible people. I recognized about 10 names.

"I'll call you back if I find out who it is," Marion said.

CHAPTER 4

Bryce

Sam got back from his trip a little before nine that night. He hugged Mom and gave Ashley and me a pat on the shoulder. Dylan ran into his arms.

I wondered where he had been. I wanted to think the best about him, but I had my doubts. Who had called him before he left? Was Sam running from the police? Could he have been involved with the gold robbery? It seemed far-fetched, but Sam had taken us to see the gold display. Then he had acted mad at the store owner, who was involved with the heist.

Mom trusted him. But don't they say love is blind? Maybe she didn't want to face the truth.

"How was your trip?" I said on the way to pick up my ATV.

"Okay," Sam said in his deep, gravelly voice.

"Where'd you go?"

"Had to fly to the East Coast."

"You flew somebody else?"

"No. Just me."

"Who'd you see?"

"People I used to work with."

Sam wasn't giving me anything. Finally, he stopped the truck by the gym and turned off the ignition. "Bryce, I want to tell you everything, but I can't. Hopefully I'll be able to soon. You're gonna have to trust me."

We got the ATV in the back of the truck and climbed in.

Something banged at the back of the gym. Sam turned on his brights, and I saw a man in a green coat running for the gulley behind the building.

"That's the guy, Sam!" I said. "Call the police!"

CHAPTER 5

Ashley

After Bryce and Sam left, I helped Mom get Dylan to bed. He likes to wear layers and layers of clothes, Bryce's and mine included. He thinks it makes him look like a football player, I guess. He still had on a lot of Band-Aids, and we couldn't get one out of his hair, so he went to sleep wearing his little Band-Aid hat and Bryce's baseball jersey from last year.

We moved to my room and Mom sat on my bed. Ever since I've had my seizures, I've loved it when she just sits with me. We can talk about almost anything—except what I wanted to talk about most: Sam.

"Mom, what did Sam mean when he said he killed Dad?"

She smoothed the bedspread. "All I know is that he's a good man. And I'd rather let him talk to you when the time's right."

I rolled my eyes. "When will the time ever be right? It'll take 20 years."

"Sam wants us all to be safe. That's all."

I had no idea what she was talking about.

She picked up a book from my bedside table and scanned the back cover. Mom's always looking at what other people write. "You ready for Friday night?"

The elementary school had recently gone through No TV Week, and as a prize to kids who turned off the tube, the organizers had planned a sleepover at the school. The principal, Mrs. Genloe, asked Mom to read a story to the kids and wondered if Bryce and I would help with the event.

"Think they'll still have it if they haven't caught the attacker?" I said.

"I hope so. I've been working on a short story."

"About what?"

She winked. "Wait and see."

CHAPTER 6

Bryce

Sam phoned the police, but I thought I saw him hesitate as he dialed. Was he afraid of something?

Since we didn't know whether the man had a gun, Sam said we shouldn't follow him. When the police got to the gym, an officer in a dark blue uniform with the words *City of Red Rock* on a patch on his sleeve took a flashlight and looked behind the building. He seemed young for a police officer and eager, like a pup who thinks he's being taken for a walk. I mean, the officer didn't wag his tail—he just had that look.

"Saw footprints," the officer said when he returned, "but he could be anywhere." He pointed to the interstate in the distance. "If he makes it there, he could hitch a ride to Denver or Colorado Springs."

Sam said the man was wearing a green jacket, had brown hair to his shoulders, and wore jeans and hiking boots. I hadn't seen all that.

"Think this is the guy who assaulted those girls?" I said.

The officer scratched his cheek. "Possible, son."

He radioed in the information and asked for a tracking dog. Sliding behind the wheel of a squad car that said *Proud to Serve* on the door, he thanked us for our help. "If you see anything else suspicious, give us a call."

CHAPTER 7

❀ Ashley ❀

Bryce and I waited for the bus at the end of our driveway. The sky was dark, like our moods. We had searched through the newspaper but found only a tiny story about the attack.

We weren't happy about not being able to ride our ATVs. We always rode them unless it was raining or had snowed a few feet. The news said it might snow, like it does a lot here in April. If it did, we wouldn't feel so bad.

When we got on the bus I could tell some kids were surprised to see me. Marion sat near the back.

"Find out anything?" I said.

She pulled out a sheet of paper with several names on it. "These kids live near town and probably walk."

I leaned over and read. Most were eighth graders, but there were a few in Bryce's and my grade, seventh, and a couple of sixth graders.

"Somebody said the girls died last night," Marion said.

I could barely get my breath. "Died?"

The kids in front of me turned around, and Marion made a face. "Shh," she whispered. "I heard the guy tried to kidnap them and when they wouldn't get in his car, he ran over them."

That hadn't been in the paper or on the radio.

A police cruiser sat outside the school, and the drop-off area for kids getting rides was packed. Inside, a poster directed everyone to the auditorium. I couldn't remember the last time that had happened.

When everyone got there, the principal, Mr. Forster, walked stiff-legged to the microphone. He has a kind face and light brown hair, blue eyes, and a goatee. He limps—Marion said he'd been probed by aliens—and each time he saw me in the hall he said hello and remembered my name. When Bryce and I first moved to Red Rock, he had told us how sorry he was that our father had died and that he would do anything he could to make our years at the school good ones.

"Good morning, students," he began. "As most of you heard, two of your classmates were attacked yesterday as they walked home from school. I want you to know that you are all safe, and we'll make sure you remain that way."

Teachers stood along the walls, watching over us like mother hens.

"You will see a police officer here throughout the day," Mr. Forster continued. "He's here for your protection."

Someone raised a hand and asked if the police had caught the guy.

"No, but the students are at the station trying to identify him."

So much for their having been run over.

"Who are they?" someone said.

Mr. Forster frowned. "We're not saying. I'm sure you can understand how tough this has been for both of them."

When the assembly was over, everyone moved to their lockers like zombies. I don't usually feel this way, but I couldn't wait to get to band.

CHAPTER 8

Bryce

Our band director, Mr. Scarberry, was late, so kids were chattering all over the place. One said the two girls had been beaten up and had lots of bruises. Others said they knew who the girls were but weren't allowed to tell. Skeeter Messler, who has a thing for my sister, handed Ashley a fresh tulip. It looked like one of the flowers that grew outside the building.

"I'm glad it wasn't you," Skeeter said.

"Thanks," Ashley said, looking like she was trying to smile.

I knew she hated the attention, but the guy just couldn't help himself. He treated her like a princess. I wanted to shake him and say, "Hello? This is Ashley! She burps and picks broccoli out of her teeth!" But I knew that wouldn't stop him. He seemed in a trance every time he was around her.

Mr. Scarberry finally walked in with a cup of steaming coffee and said hello to each section of the band. As usual, he opened his black book and called roll. When he came to Tracy Elliot's name, he stopped, put the pencil to his tongue, made a mark, and moved on.

Everybody knew Tracy was a party girl. She was last chair in a long line of clarinets, even behind Skeeter, who was affectionately called Squeaker by the other woodwinds. Tracy hung around with an eighth grader named Cammy Michaels, and their parents let them stay all day at the bowling alley, the arcade, or the Chapel Hills Mall in Colorado Springs. I guessed they were the ones who had been attacked.

CHAPTER 9

❦ Ashley ❦

Usually you heard people laughing and telling jokes in the cafeteria, but at lunch it felt like someone had replaced our Twinkies with lima beans. Kids whispered. Soda cans popped and paper bags crackled.

"I knew it," Marion said, pulling from her brown bag an apple she said had been grown organically. "Cammy and Tracy do everything together."

"Still think they're dead?" I said, knowing Mr. Forster wouldn't lie about their being at the police station.

Marion shrugged. "They have to notify the next of kin before they can tell us. I say the guy took off with them."

Hayley sat next to me.

"This guy could be an alien," Marion said.

Hayley rolled her eyes.

"Seriously, I've read about people being abducted right out of their houses and taken up to spaceships. I'll bet the girls don't even remember half of what happened. . . ."

As Marion continued, Mr. Forster walked in. I stood and he nodded. "Ashley," he said.

"Mr. Forster, people are talking about Cammy and Tracy." He didn't seem surprised. "I've heard everything from them being beaten up to them actually being dead."

He shook his head and chuckled. "I met with the victims this morning. They're shaken up, of course, but I expect they'll be back at school tomorrow."

"So it *is* Cammy and Tracy?"

Mr. Forster looked at his watch. "Lunch is almost over, Ms. Timberline."

CHAPTER 10

Bryce

The day dragged as we waited for news. Coach Baldwin ran us guys to death in gym class, getting us ready for our time trials in the mile.

I nearly fell asleep in English class and would have if Mrs. Ferguson hadn't decided to tell us a spooky short story about a teenage girl who decides to run away with some guy in a car.

"Good literature—stories—help us make sense of what's going on around us," she said. "Some great stories have come out of terrible circumstances."

This was all leading to something I wasn't sure I liked. Mrs.

Ferguson glanced at her watch. "Think about something bad that's happened to you. Make up a character, give him or her a name, and change that story's outcome. You'll read your stories aloud tomorrow in class."

Only one thing came to *my* mind. My dad.

CHAPTER 11

❀ Ashley ❀

Just before English was over, Mr. Forster made an announcement over the PA system that he wanted everyone to exit at the front of the building. There are a million doors in our school, so going out only in the front means lots of crowding and pushing. I figured the guy who had attacked the two girls was still loose.

Bryce and I can make it home in about 10 minutes on our ATVs, but when we ride the bus we have to go to the high school and take the long way home up Red Rock Hill, so it's an extra 45 minutes.

I wrote my story on the way, imagining that on the day Dad went on his trip I had spilled cereal on his suit and he had to change. Then

I had a bike accident as he was backing out of the driveway, and he had to help me. I kept doing dumb things, and he kept getting delayed until he missed his flight.

The last line of my story read, "On the day all the planes in the world were told to stay on the ground, my father came home and hugged me for saving his life."

I wished it were true.

Then I thought about Sam and his confession. I hoped I didn't have another story to tell.

CHAPTER 12

Bryce

When I found out Ashley had written her story about Dad, I tore up what I had written. It was only two sentences, but I made a big deal about it, acting angry and hurt. Our upcoming basketball game was against Coronado, a team that had barely beaten us the last time. I could write about that.

But I didn't.

I put off writing and played video games upstairs in the barn. Sam has an office there and an exercise room where he lets us play games and walk on the treadmill or lift weights.

I was in there alone when Sam's phone rang, and his answering machine picked up.

My heart thumped as the beep sounded. I hit the Pause button on my game and strained to hear the message.

A fast-talking man said, "Sam . . . have to get used to that. It's Tim in D.C. Just making sure you got back okay. Hope things are going better for you." The man paused. "Look, we've been talking about your situation. This is the kind of thing we were concerned about when you started this new family. The director thinks it's best you keep as much information as you can to yourself. If we have to move you again, we'll make it happen. Good seeing you again. Been a long time. Take care."

CHAPTER 13

❀ Ashley ❀

That night on the phone Hayley said her mother saw Cammy and Tracy going into the Toot Toot Café at about noon. That seemed odd, unless the police were taking them to eat.

Mom kept the house locked tight during the day. Even our dogs, Pippin and Frodo, seemed skittish, milling around the back door and whining. When I let them out, they went as far as the invisible fence allowed and stuck their noses in the air.

Sam said if the police hadn't caught the guy by now, whoever it was had probably gotten away—maybe by hopping a freight train. The guy could have headed north to Denver, bought a bus ticket, and could be anywhere.

Still, Mom and Sam wouldn't let us ride our ATVs to school, and the local Girl Scout troop canceled its meeting. Leigh wanted to practice driving and get more night hours so she could get her license, but Sam had left to take Dylan for a haircut and Mom said she didn't want to be out after dark.

Leigh stomped to her room and slammed the door. I felt bad for her, having lost her mom and little sister in the same plane crash that killed my dad. I could tell she was trying hard to like Bryce and me, but she wasn't trying hard enough, if you know what I mean. I couldn't help feeling that Bryce and I were just one of the inconveniences in her life.

I read a little in my Bible before I went to sleep. I try to read something out of it every day, but I don't always. Tonight it was a passage in Luke 10. Jesus had just said you have to love your neighbor as yourself, and an expert in the law asked him, "Who is my neighbor?"

Jesus said:

> *"A Jewish man was traveling on a trip from Jerusalem to Jericho, and he was attacked by bandits. They stripped him of his clothes, beat him up, and left him half dead beside the road.*
>
> *"By chance a priest came along. But when he saw the man lying there, he crossed to the other side of the road and passed him by. A Temple assistant walked over and looked at him lying there, but he also passed by on the other side.*
>
> *"Then a despised Samaritan came along, and when he saw the man, he felt compassion for him. Going over to him, the Samaritan soothed his wounds with olive oil and wine and bandaged them. Then he put the man on his own donkey and took him to an inn, where he took care of him.*

The next day he handed the innkeeper two silver coins, telling him, 'Take care of this man. If his bill runs higher than this, I'll pay you the next time I'm here.'

"Now which of these three would you say was a neighbor to the man who was attacked by bandits?" Jesus asked.

The man replied, "The one who showed him mercy."

Then Jesus said, "Yes, now go and do the same."

I've heard a whole lot of sermons about this guy, the Good Samaritan, but it struck me tonight that Jesus was like this man. He didn't have to come to earth and help us, but he did. He must have felt deep pity for us because we were so trapped by our sins. And he paid a lot more than just money to help us—he paid with his own life.

I wrote in my journal:

> I want to be like the Good Samaritan, full of love and compassion. So much that I don't think about myself but about others. God, help me be like this guy and do something, even at school tomorrow.

You have to be careful what you pray for, because God just might take you up on it.

CHAPTER 14

Bryce

I wrote my story during lunch the next day—at least I tried to write it. Words don't come as quickly for me as they do for Ashley. She takes more after Mom, I guess. When I write a story or an essay, choosing words is like picking blackberries. I have to reach in and avoid the thorns, wondering if there's a snake back there somewhere, and when I'm sure it's okay, I write one down.

I named my character Chet Becker, because I'd known a kid with that name in Illinois, and I had him sink every shot he took. By the end of the story, Chet had scored 70 points and had 20 steals.

What had really happened to me wasn't that spectacular. It was actually awful. You should know that I'm not a great athlete. I'm kind of dorky looking, with long arms and gangly legs, but Sam told me about this guy named Larry Bird who used to play for the Boston Celtics. Sam said Bird looked like somebody taken right off the farm, but when they put a basketball in his hands he knew what to do. That's how I wanted to play.

Anyway, our team had fought Coronado the whole game, trying to keep them from getting the ball to their big man, #23. We were down only a point with 17 seconds left when #23 clunked one off the rim and I got the rebound. I threw the ball to Duncan Swift, and he brought it across half-court and called a time-out. Now we had 13 seconds.

Coach Baldwin called a play and told me to throw the ball inbounds. Everybody on the court and in the stands knew Duncan was going to take the shot, because he's our best player. It was my job to throw it to him and get in position in case Coronado double- or triple-teamed him.

After the buzzer sounded, the ref handed me the ball and started his five count. Duncan gave a head fake and darted into the backcourt, and I tossed him the ball. But he didn't turn when I expected, and the ball bounced off his shoulder and into the hands of a Coronado player. It took six seconds for me to catch the guy and foul him. He sank both shots, and there was only enough time for a desperation heave at the end, which Duncan almost made.

The coach tried to make us feel better in the locker room, but I could hardly breathe. Everybody patted me on the back and said I had a good game, but I knew I'd blown it. I couldn't wait until the next time we'd meet, coming up Saturday.

CHAPTER 15

✾ Ashley ✾

"Look who's here," Marion said as Cammy and Tracy walked into the lunchroom. Immediately a group of girls gathered. Marion jumped up and glanced back at me. "Aren't you coming?"

It was like a rock concert. The only thing missing was the fainting. I could hear the girls talking several tables away.

"We thought you were dead."

"Where were you?"

"How did it happen?"

"Were you scared?"

"How'd you get away?"

Mr. Forster came through and shooed everyone away, but as soon as he was gone, the noise returned with whispers, then got louder and louder.

A few minutes later Marion returned.

"Attacked by aliens?" I said.

"No, they said it was the guy who sits outside the Toot Toot. The weird one with the army jacket and stringy hair."

I knew him. He sat in a rocking chair on the wooden sidewalk and slept or read. Once I saw him scribbling on paper as I walked by. He smelled like a wet animal—I guess because he slept outside—and I was surprised someone didn't ask him to move.

"What did he do?"

Marion scooted closer. "Cammy said he grabbed them both by the wrists when they were headed home. He pulled them behind the row of shops next to the Toot Toot and into an old shed back there. He put duct tape on their hands and feet."

"Why would he do that?"

Marion shrugged. "They said he was mumbling at them, real angry. Then he left, and they got away before he came back."

Cammy and Tracy aren't my two favorite people on the planet, but I felt sorry for them. That would have given me nightmares forever.

"The police have given the guy's picture to the media," Marion said. "I guess he was arrested before."

Cammy and Tracy had a new group of kids around them and seemed to be telling their story again and again.

CHAPTER 16

Bryce

"Very good, Bryce," Mrs. Ferguson said after I read my story. I don't like writing as much as Ashley does, but I love getting up in front of the class.

Ashton was next. He wrote about his pet ferret Freddy, which in real life had been run over by his older brother. I was there when it happened. Ashton tried to revive the poor thing, but it's hard to give a ferret CPR. We buried him in Ashton's backyard and put a cross over the little grave with an inscription, "Here lies Freddy, a faithful ferret." Ashton said it was good alliteration.

In his story, the ferret grew up to become president of "Ferretica" and was interviewed by Larry King. Everybody laughed at the wild things Freddy did, but I could tell Ashton still missed the animal.

"Very nice fantasy, Ashton," Mrs. Ferguson said. "It fits with what I asked you to do."

"Fantasy?" Ashton said.

"Well, let's face it—it pushes the boundaries of believability."

Ashton trudged back to his seat. "It could happen."

Next up was Jeff Alexander. Adults call him "inspiring" because he's fighting cancer, but I just call him my friend. Last year he looked like any other kid in sixth grade. Now he has only a little hair, has to have someone help him carry his books to class, and is a lot thinner. A couple of years ago his doctors found some kind of tumor, and he went through chemotherapy and surgeries and stuff.

But all these things just make it more fun to hear him talk, because he has a great sense of humor. His diary is published every month in the school newspaper. He talks about what it's like to have cancer, but somehow every one of his columns makes you laugh.

His story was titled "The Day I Found My Hair." Instead of going through chemotherapy and losing his hair, his story was about a day he had chemo and grew more hair than he could handle.

By the end of the story, he had grown so much hair that he had to shave his body every day, and he used the extra to power all of Colorado for one year. "I not only became a handsome spokesman for the Hair-Energy Commission, but I also provided the electricity for everyone's hair dryers!"

I slapped Jeff a high five as he sat down next to me and I was laughing so hard that I didn't realize Ashley was at the front of the class.

CHAPTER 17

❀ Ashley ❀

Sweat trickled down my arm as I looked out over the other kids' faces. They were still giggling at Jeff's story.

Bryce may not get nervous in front of the class, but I sure do. I don't know why. It was just a stupid story. I tried to act calm, which only made my paper shake. I hate when that happens.

Everybody laughed when I did dumb things that held Dad up in my story. Mrs. Ferguson seemed perplexed. Every other story had shown kids (and ferrets) doing superhuman things—winning skateboard competitions, catching gigantic fish, and playing professional sports. My story was the only one where a kid actually messed up.

When I got to the end and my dad hugged me, some kids gasped. Everyone knew what had really happened to him. Mrs. Ferguson just stared at her desk while I returned to my seat.

Bryce smiled.

CHAPTER 18

◎ *Bryce* ◎

On Thursdays, either Ashley or I go to the counselor at our church. Mrs. Ogilvie has been talking with us ever since Mom started going to Mountain View Chapel. A lot of people call counselors "shrinks" and think you have to lie on a couch or let them hook probes to your brain. But we just talk.

Mrs. Ogilvie's office is on the side of the church with the best view of the mountains. We started the session like we always do, with me picking out a piece of candy from a jar on her desk. That makes me feel like a little boy, but I kind of feel like that anyway, talking about my dad.

Sometimes Mrs. Ogilvie tells stories about when she was a kid.

Her father died when she was 10, and she says that affected her like nothing else.

When I first started going, I worried she would ask personal questions, but she just gets me to talk. A lot of times she'll ask, "How did that make you feel?"

This week I talked about Boo Heckler, because the week before he tried to bully me. I told her a little about Gold Town, but I didn't tell her everything.

Before the hour ended—it always goes really fast—she asked me what I knew about the attack at school.

I told her I didn't know the girls but that everybody seemed scared. "Ashley and I hate that we can't ride our ATVs to school."

Mrs. Ogilvie smiled. "That would dampen my day too." Then her face scrunched up, the same way it did when I told her about how we found out my dad had died.

"Something wrong?" I said.

"I know the young man who's been accused," she said. "His parents used to come to this church. They asked me to talk to Danny right after his . . . well, I just can't imagine him doing something like that."

It was the first time I had heard anyone use his name. "Danny what?"

"Ingram. He's such a bright young man. He'd spend hours at the Garden of the Gods, drawing the rock formations, climbing them."

"What happened to him?"

Mrs. Ogilvie closed her notebook and smiled. I figured she couldn't say. "Let's just say his parents have been worried." She pulled out a calendar and scheduled my next visit for three weeks later. "I'm going to be away next week at a conference in Chicago. Can I bring you back anything?"

I thought about the restaurant in Chicago that serves the best barbecued-pork sandwich and coleslaw. Dad used to take us there. But I shook my head.

CHAPTER 19

❦ Ashley ❦

When Mom got back from the church with Bryce, she asked him and me to get some meat from the freezer below Sam's office in the barn. Sometimes it snows a lot and we can't get out of our house for days, so they always keep a good supply.

Bryce noticed the muddy footprints first. They went inside and up to Sam's office.

"Did you lock the door after you were done in there?" I said.

"Of course. I always lock it." But I could tell that Bryce was nervous. Sam gets ticked when he finds the door unlocked.

Bryce led the way up the stairs and tried the knob. It turned.

"What if someone's in there?" I whispered.

"We'll surprise them," Bryce said. "Be ready to run."

Bryce burst in, yelling at the top of his lungs. There was no one in the exercise room. He turned on the light to the bathroom. Nothing. The door to Sam's office was open a crack.

Bryce raised his voice. "Have the squad cars pull around the back." I was sure he wouldn't fool anyone. Bryce thinks his voice is a lot lower than it really is.

Bryce kicked the door open, and it banged off the water cooler in the corner. Nothing seemed out of place, except for the small refrigerator underneath Sam's desk. It stood open and empty. Sam kept it stocked with soda, fruit, and his special coffee beans. (In the morning his office smells like one of those big bookstores.) A garbage can had been turned over, and the bag was missing.

"Who would steal sodas?" I said.

Leigh's boyfriend, Randy, had been around, but would he steal something from Sam's office?

"What about Boo?" I said. "He must know where we live."

A sick look came over Bryce's face.

We ran to tell Mom about the break-in, and she phoned Sam. He said he was on his way home and not to call the police.

"Why not?" Bryce said.

Mom wiped her hands on a towel. "I have to get the meat."

CHAPTER 20

Bryce

After Sam got home, I dogged him to the barn with a flashlight and showed him the muddy footprints. Pippin and Frodo followed us into the yard, bristling and barking. Ashley stood at the back door and called them inside.

Upstairs, Sam inspected his office and the refrigerator. He agreed that whoever it was had loaded things up in the garbage bag. "I had a couple of sandwiches in there too," Sam said.

"Why didn't you want to call the police?"

He stroked his whiskers, which cast a shadow on his face, even though he had shaved in the morning. Sam's hair looked a little grayer these days, and his eyes seemed tired.

Before he could answer I said, "Is it the same reason you don't want us talking about what happened at Gold Town?"

Sam glanced around the room. "I just don't think we should involve them. Not yet. It's probably some kid. Whoever it was could have taken the ATVs or computers. Strange." He locked the barn on our way out and put a hand on my shoulder. "We'll sic the hounds on them if they come back."

If Ashley was right and this whole thing was Boo Heckler's work, he was sure to be back.

CHAPTER 21

❀ Ashley ❀

I tried to get some rest after school Friday with the sleepover coming up that night, but I couldn't. Sometimes reading helps, but I was so gripped by the book I was reading that it kept me up. That and Pippin and Frodo barking.

Mom drove Bryce and me to the elementary school later that afternoon. Parents and leaders had a pre-sleepover meeting, complete with pizza and sub sandwiches. The kids would arrive in an hour.

The principal, Mrs. Genloe, had several things planned. The kids would eat when they arrived at six. At seven, a clown would perform (which made Bryce roll his eyes). Mrs. Genloe said the clown had trained pigs that did tricks. Then Mom would tell her story.

"And we have a special presentation on safety by a surprise duo," the principal said. "With all the talk about the assault, we don't want to brush this under the rug."

"What about the bonfire?" somebody asked.

Mrs. Genloe frowned. "Because of the assault, we won't be having our annual bonfire."

Between 9 and 11 the climbing wall, an inflatable jumping castle, dodgeball, and other games would be set up in the gym. At 11, the kids would have a scavenger hunt throughout the school, with prizes awarded. Each class had selected a video to watch at midnight. Then it would be lights-out.

Just before six, we got our assignments. Bryce would be with the third-grade boys.

I was the last helper to get an assignment. Mrs. Genloe took me aside. "We have a fifth grader we'd like you to keep an eye on."

"Just one?"

"Wally is a little slower than the rest and has been known to wander. It would help if you'd stay with him until midnight. Can you do that?"

I looked out the window at a little boy with thick glasses. He wore a Colorado Rockies jersey, a pair of Avalanche sweats, a Broncos hat, and a smile a mile wide. His full backpack bounced as he walked. I wondered if Mom had told Mrs. Genloe that I might want to be a special ed teacher when I grew up.

CHAPTER 22

Bryce

The third-grade class was a blast. Out of 23 kids, only 12 had made it through No TV Week without watching (or so they had said). Everybody wore a name tag with their room number. I helped pass out the pizza. One boy, Darrel, said he didn't like pizza, so his mother had packed carrots and celery. I ran to the cafeteria and found an untouched sub sandwich. Darrel's eyes grew round as hot air balloons. When I gave it to him, I figured I had made at least one friend for the night.

Red Rock Elementary is a flat, one-story brick building half the size of the middle school but twice as confusing. It kind of looks like the Pentagon, with five entrances for the different grades. In the middle is a combination library/auditorium, where special speakers talk to the kids. The fenced-in playground is outside a back door, and you have to walk outside across the playground to get to the gymnasium.

You'd think it would be easy to figure out where to go, but if you're not careful, the hallways are like a maze, with curious trails that lead to dead ends and doors that open to spooky unused rooms.

I've worked in the church nursery, so it wasn't hard to figure out that the adult leaders wanted me to blend in and help. When they asked me to get something, I asked Darrel to point the way.

After the clown came, one of the adults said I could take a break. What a relief! I hate clowns. I wandered down the hall to wait for Mom and noticed the technology room. The computers were awesome.

I sat at a computer hooked up to the Internet and put my fingers over the keys. I remembered the guy on Sam's answering machine. He had said a lot of things I didn't understand, but one thing stood out. *"Sam . . . have to get used to that."* What did he mean?

I typed in *Samuel Timberline* on a search engine, and a bunch of things came up. A water well survey in Louisiana, a bus route in Texas, a magazine with features about the sawmill industry, but no Sam Timberline—as in stepfather of Ashley and Bryce.

I went to another site where you could look up phone numbers and addresses and typed in our home number. The computer stared at me like I had digital bad breath. Finally, it came back with an error message. I typed in Sam's office phone number, and the same message popped up. I typed in our address and the message said, "No information for that listing."

Strange.

I typed in our nearest neighbor's information, and it popped up like lightning. Every house around us came back with complete listings. Every house except ours.

I heard applause in the auditorium and shut down the computer. I hoped the clown was finished.

CHAPTER 23

❀ Ashley ❀

Wally clapped and giggled at the clown—Ding-Dong—whose big trick was to pull balloons out of his nose by pushing a button that made a doorbell sound. He then blew the balloons into animal shapes and passed them out.

Ding-Dong tripped on his oversized shoes and fell. I thought Wally was going to split his sides laughing. The rest of the kids clapped politely as Mrs. Genloe helped Ding-Dong up. The clown pulled her down with him, and Ping-Pong balls fell out of his hat. He held up a sign: Ding-Dong's Ping-Pongs.

Finally, a whipped-cream pie came out, and the kids whooped. I could tell Mrs. Genloe knew the drill by the way she moved away from it, but the kids thought it was real. When Ding-Dong slipped again and let go of the pie, Mrs. Genloe ducked and the beloved gym teacher (wearing a plastic bag over his clothes) took the pie full in the face. The kids laughed wildly, pointed at him, and screamed when he shook his head like a dog and sent whipped cream flying.

Wally rolled on the floor and stomped his feet. His face turned red.

Ding-Dong brought out his trained pigs that had been on some late-night show doing tricks. I felt bad for Mom having to follow an act like this, but that's show business.

Mrs. Genloe had everyone stand and stretch after Ding-Dong gave a final ring of his bell and left. Then she introduced Mom as a successful author who lived in the area. She mentioned Bryce—who wasn't there—and pointed me out. Wally looked up at me like I was some kind of a celebrity.

I got nervous. Mom didn't have orange hair, balloons coming out of her nose, whipped-cream pies, or dancing pigs. She just had a few pages in her lap.

CHAPTER 24

Bryce

The room got really quiet when Mom began, especially after the laughing and squealing over the clown.

"I want to read a scary part of a new story I'm working on for kids," Mom said. "The main characters are twins, and they live right here in Red Rock."

Kids looked at each other, and the one Ashley was watching pointed at me and nodded.

"This chapter is called 'Underwater.'"

As soon as she started, I realized this was really our story about being chased by robbers near Gold Town. She made the reservoir into a river and changed lots of stuff, but I knew where the idea came from. When the car went into the water, you could've heard whipped cream dripping from the gym teacher's face. A couple of kids put their hands over their eyes.

Mom and Sam had told us we couldn't tell anyone about that weekend, how our SUV had plunged into the water and we almost drowned. Now Mom was telling it in a story! That didn't seem fair, but something about it also felt great.

There was a lot more screaming in the real crash, and the dad in Mom's story had time to give the kids instructions and tell them when to hold their breath, but the whole thing made me scared again. You don't survive an event like that and not have it affect you big-time.

The water was just about up to their chins when Mom put the pages down and said, "That's as far as I've gotten."

The kids wailed that it wasn't fair to leave them hanging, so Mom smiled and pulled a crumpled piece of paper from her pocket. "Well, this is one of the drafts I threw away, but if you'd like."

CHAPTER 25

❀ Ashley ❀

By the time Mom finished, she had the twins on a rock in the middle of the river. Even the teachers and parents seemed to hang on every word. Mom stopped without saying if their father made it out of the car with their little brother, but I could tell if Mom ever had it published it would be a hit.

Someone raised a hand. "Is that true?"

Mom smiled. "That's the fun of making up stories. It doesn't have to be true. But if it feels like it could happen, and if it touches you somewhere down here—" she put a hand over her heart—"you know it's a good story."

"How do you come up with your ideas?" another kid said.

Mom looked at me and winked. "I let my imagination run."

A girl near Wally whispered, "I think it would be cool to have a writer for a mother, don't you?"

"That's what I want to be when I grow up," another said.

Everybody clapped for Mom. She waved good-bye to me, and Bryce walked her to the front door.

"Is everyone having a good time?" Mrs. Genloe shouted.

The kids screamed and put fists in the air.

"We almost didn't have this get-together tonight. We almost had to cancel. Does anyone know why?"

"The attack!" a boy yelled.

"Those two girls," a girl said.

"The guy is still on the loose," another said.

Mrs. Genloe nodded. "Well, we thought this would be a good opportunity to learn some safety tips. So I'd like you to welcome three guests. Actually, four."

A police officer walked down the hall with a dog at his side. The boys went wild. The girls *ooh*ed and *aah*ed at the dog.

Mrs. Genloe held up a hand. "You've all heard different things about what happened that day, haven't you? Let's talk about what really happened."

The kids gasped as Cammy Michaels and Tracy Elliot walked onto the stage.

CHAPTER 26

Bryce

Cammy was thin with long blonde hair, and her skin was the color of the inside of pancakes. Tracy's hair was almost black with red streaks around the sides of her face. She wore dark jeans and had several earrings. Both wore lots of makeup—red lips, dark eyelids, that kind of thing. Makeup is okay, I guess, but some people wind up looking less beautiful and more like Ding-Dong, if you know what I mean.

The police officer let the girls sit on stools. The dog obeyed every command, and I figured the leash was to protect it from the kids rather than the other way around. I was glad Ding-Dong's pigs were gone, because the dog looked hungry.

Cammy took the microphone, looked at Tracy, and stifled a laugh. I figured she was nervous because a lot of people do that when they're in front of a crowd. Tracy nudged her, and Cammy went limp-wristed with the microphone, letting it drift away from her mouth. The police officer stepped forward and pushed it closer.

"Okay, so I'm supposed to tell you what happened to us the other day," Cammy began. "I'm sure you've all heard about it. We had stayed a little later after school to get some help with homework." She giggled. "We need all the help we can get. Anyway"—(snort)—"we were coming home from school, just passing the café, when this guy jumps out and grabs us around our necks. He dragged us behind the café to a little shed. We were both really scared."

Tracy took the microphone. "He had duct tape back there—you know, the big gray rolls you see at the hardware store. And before we knew it, he taped over our mouths and tied our wrists together. We tried to scream, but it all happened so fast that I guess nobody heard us."

The kids stared, and parents stood at the back shaking their heads. Everybody got as quiet as they had for Mom's story. Several mothers had hands over their mouths as the girls continued.

"Please, you guys have to be careful," Cammy said in a high-pitched voice. "If we'd have been aware of what was going on around us and not talking to each other, we would have seen trouble coming. We could have crossed the street and avoided that guy or yelled for help."

"Fortunately, we were able to get away before the guy came back or he might have really hurt us," Tracy said. "So we hope you'll all learn from our mistake and stay safe. Red Rock is not that big of a place. But it only takes one bad guy to mess everything up."

CHAPTER 27

❀ Ashley ❀

I watched Cammy and Tracy as they moved away from the microphone.

The kids all applauded and several raised their hands.

"Did you call the police right away?"

"Did you get to ride in a squad car?"

"Have they caught the guy?"

"Did you pick him out of a lineup like on TV?"

The girls went back to the microphone and answered questions until Mrs. Genloe returned. She thanked the two, then introduced the officer, a dark-skinned man with a mustache. While he talked he kept his radio on, so we heard all the chatter.

Tracy and Cammy moved to the back of the auditorium where several parents hugged them and the girls smiled. Something bothered me about their story, but I couldn't put a finger on what it was.

I knelt to ask Wally what he thought of the policeman and his dog. Wally's balloon made by Ding-Dong lay on the floor, but Wally was gone.

CHAPTER 28

Bryce

Just when the policeman was getting to the part about how to spot people who might hurt you, Ashley darted down a hallway and disappeared.

I ran to catch up and finally found her in one of the classrooms. Her eyes were red and her hands shook.

"Wally's gone," she said. "He was right in front of me, but now he's gone."

"He's gotta be around somewhere."

"Bryce, they gave me one thing to do the entire night and I blew it. What if he's outside? What if that guy gets him? What if he gets hit by a car? It's all my fault!"

"Calm down. We'll get everybody to help us—"

"No, we can't let them know I lost him."

I found the nearest bathroom and checked all the stalls. I skirted the auditorium and checked another bathroom on the other side. Nothing.

I found Ashley again and shook my head. "I'll go to the playground. You look in here."

She nodded. "Be careful."

CHAPTER 29

❀ Ashley ❀

I went to the auditorium to make sure Wally hadn't tried to get closer to the dog. I moved behind the adults, looking between shoulders, scanning the stage and seats.

How could I have been so stupid! I thought. *He could have slipped away anytime in the last half hour. He could be in Colorado Springs by now!*

Mrs. Ogilvie had told me that it's important to think about what you say to yourself. Sounds kind of funny, and at first I thought only crazy people talked to themselves, but now I know better. If you keep calling yourself stupid, it wears you down.

"Okay, I'm not stupid," I whispered, frantically looking in the girls' bathroom. "I didn't mean to lose him. It was just a mistake. All I have to do is stay calm and—"

Something moved in the corner.

"Wally?"

The stall opened. It was Cammy. "Who are you talking to?"

My heart sank. "I was just looking for someone."

"You're the Timberline girl, right?" Cammy said. "The twin."

"Yeah."

"Who are you looking for?"

I told her, my voice shaking. "He must have took off when you and Tracy were speaking."

I hoped she would help, but she scowled. "Kid's probably scared to death, wandering around this dungeon." She walked past me. "Glad I'm not you."

Wally could be dead by now, and it was my fault.

CHAPTER 30

Bryce

I let the outside door close and heard the clunk of the latch behind me. That sent my stomach (full of sub sandwich) to my ankles. All the school doors were locked. Unless Ashley came for me, I was stuck.

The parking lot looked like an SUV convention. Ski racks. Bike racks. It's part of living in Colorado. The temperature had reached 70 that day, but the wind had picked up and the evening temperature dropped. The night air felt cool compared to inside. When we go to Rockies games, we always take blankets. Sometimes it even snows at the stadium.

The stars shone bright, and the quarter moon looked like God had hung it there.

My first thought was to call out for Wally, but I held back. If the little guy was hiding for some reason, he'd never answer.

Something moved at the edge of the playground. The overhead lights cast an eerie shadow on the swings and basketball hoops. A dark animal padded past the monkey bars and four-square boxes. A fox. They ran through our town like squirrels.

I stepped forward as the fox ran down a hill and across the soccer field. In the distance I saw the moonlit cap of Pikes Peak, white as a snow cone. The Front Range blocked most of the 14,000-foot mountain, but you could see the top from just about anywhere.

I scanned the playground again and heard what I imagined was Wally banging against something metal. I raced around front to find an American flag flapping in the breeze, the rope and metal clips knocking against the flagpole.

"Wally?" I said, loud enough to echo off the building.

Something rustled the bushes by the front door.

I froze, trying not to breathe. What if the guy who attacked the girls wanted to shut them up and had followed them here?

My voice shook. "Wally, is that you?"

CHAPTER 31

❀ Ashley ❀

I looked in vacant rooms before returning to the auditorium. Sleeping bags and pillows were piled in corners and near closets. It's weird how something as normal as a school looks creepy in the dark.

The police officer introduced Max, the sniffer dog. Kids came forward to pet him, and I felt sorry for the poor thing. He looked at the officer with pleading eyes. If he could talk, the dog would have said, "If I can't attack anyone or find anyone, can we get out of here?" He was a beautiful dog with piercing eyes and a shiny coat.

The officer said Max was three years old and at night went home with him to his family. Max was trained to sniff out seven kinds of drugs.

"There she is," someone said, pointing at me.

Mrs. Genloe hurried over. Cammy stood with her arms crossed, whispering to some parents who looked at me like I had clubbed a baby seal.

"Ashley, where is Wally?" Mrs. Genloe said. Her voice was strained, and the wrinkles in her forehead were so deep I could have planted corn in them.

I glanced at Cammy and the group in the corner. Tracy motioned to me and shook her head.

"Uh, I was watching the police presentation, and when I looked down—"

"You lost him?" Mrs. Genloe said.

The whole auditorium grew quiet. Kids turned and looked at me. Even Max glared.

Someone banged on an outside door and kids screamed, some running for parent helpers, others huddling near the policeman. Max's ears perked up, and he stood at attention.

Someone opened the door and Bryce walked in. He looked at me and frowned.

How was I going to find Wally?

CHAPTER 32

Bryce

Ashley ran from the room, and I thought she had lost it. I was shaking from the noises outside, plus some teacher was yelling at me for leaving the building. I was about to explain when Mrs. Genloe called for quiet and asked kids to clear the aisles. "We have a situation and we need your help."

Before she could continue, Ashley rushed in holding a backpack over her head. She approached the police officer and said, "Max is a sniffer dog, right?"

The officer nodded, smiling. "He'll find your friend. Get everybody seated and quiet."

Ashley turned to the principal and the woman nodded. "Everybody listen!" Ashley said. "Wally slipped away. We're going to have Max find him, but you have to sit down!"

It was a perfect idea. Almost as if Ashley and the policeman had planned it. The entire group hushed and sat with a whomp.

The cop knelt and held the backpack down to Max. The dog sniffed it from top to bottom, prancing in place like he couldn't wait to get started. "Go get him," the officer said as he unsnapped the leash.

Max shot up the aisle, ran to the top, turned right, and went straight to the spot where Ashley and Wally had been sitting. Kids streamed from their seats to see the dog at work. Ashley was right behind the officer, and a crowd of kids followed them.

I'd never be able to catch up that way, so I went up some stairs to the main hallway. Max passed me, panting, his tongue lolling to one side. He sniffed the floor, went down a hall, circled back, and continued toward the main office.

The officer jogged after him, and I joined the chase.

CHAPTER 33

✾ Ashley ✾

When I heard Max bark, my heart leaped. A pile of jackets and blankets lay by the front door near a coatrack. Max danced over the pile, whining, his tail wagging. He spun in a circle, looked back at the officer, raised a paw, and barked again. The coats moved and Wally giggled.

The cop snapped Max's leash on with one hand and moved the coats with the other. "Good boy," he said, stroking the dog.

Wally bounded out of the coats as the kids rushed up behind us. Everyone cheered. Wally said, "You found me!" and hugged me. I was so relieved I almost cried.

As we made our way back to the auditorium one of the parents said, "This is why middle schoolers shouldn't be helping."

I felt my face turning red.

Bryce came up and said, "Good idea."

Mrs. Genloe assigned one of the parents to Wally, which was okay with me, except he kept scooting away and running to find me. Bryce went to his third-grade room to help set up for the movie while others went to the gym.

I heard a honk outside and pulled back a curtain. Cammy and Tracy ran to a bright red sports car, and it didn't look like something a mom or dad would drive. Cammy spotted me, laughed, and shook her head, which made me want Max to take a bite out of crime—if you know what I mean.

CHAPTER 34

◎ *Bryce* ◎

The next morning I woke up from two hours of sleep and found that one of the third graders had had an accident in his sleeping bag. While one of the dads took him to the bathroom to change, I hung the sleeping bag on the chain-link fence outside to dry.

Parents who had volunteered for breakfast arrived with donuts, pancake mix, orange juice, and other stuff. I saw Duncan Swift's dad and waved.

"Ready for the big game today?" Mr. Swift said. He seemed kind of young to be a father. His hair was spiked like Duncan's, and he wore blazing white tennis shoes and tight jeans. He always yelled the loudest at games and came onto the floor at halftime to tell Duncan what he was doing wrong.

"I almost forgot," I said.

He squinted and stopped. "Forgot Coronado, probably the biggest game of the year? Remember what those guys did to you last game?"

I nodded. "Yeah, I guess I am ready for some payback."

"Payback is right. Tell your dad we'll save a seat for him. Can't wait to see you guys blow them out of that gym."

Jeff Alexander struggled out of his car as his mom waved at me and carried some food into the school. Jeff had told me he wanted to spend the night with the kids like I was, but I guess he didn't have the energy.

"How'd it go last night?" he said, making it to the sidewalk and leaning on the railing.

I told him what happened, and his jaw dropped. "Wish I could have been there for that." He pushed his hat back, and I saw a little tuft of hair growing at the front of his scalp.

"Looks like your mane's growing back in."

He grinned. "I told Mom I was going to get a Mohawk once it all grew back. I think she'll actually let me do it."

"I wouldn't put it past you," I said.

"How about coming to my house tonight?" Jeff said. "Got some stuff I need to talk over. Maybe spend the night?"

CHAPTER 35

❀ Ashley ❀

Bryce went to bed as soon as Mom brought us home, but I couldn't. I had to tell her what had happened. She hugged me.

"I know I messed up letting Wally get away, but—"

"Sounds like Wally gets away a lot," Mom said.

"I don't know why they had to be so mean to me. At least Bryce helped."

She smiled. "It's nice having somebody who understands, huh?"

I went to my room and wrote in my journal everything I could remember about Cammy and Tracy's speech.

I woke up with Bryce standing by my bed, yawning. "You coming to my game?"

I rubbed my eyes and tried to stand. I like going to Bryce's games because I get to see my friends. And Duncan. But I couldn't drag myself out of bed.

"Sam's taking me," Bryce said. "You can stay here."

"If you insist," I said.

CHAPTER 36

Bryce

Sam drove me to the game against Coronado. I had slept until about 10 minutes before we left and felt like a used dishrag. I wish I could wake up as fast as Pippin and Frodo. I guess that's why adults drink so much coffee. I like the smell of the stuff, but I can't stand the taste. Unless it's one of those foofy coffee drinks—you know, the latte, frappé-whatevers. I like those.

As Sam drove, we listened to the radio and the latest about the attack on the girls. The guy's picture had been on TV and in the paper, but the police still hadn't found him.

I walked into the Coronado gym and looked for my teammates.

Another game was going on, a blowout. The Coronado team sat across from us on the bleachers, and some of them tried to stare us down. Their big guy, #23, was already over six feet tall and had arms like tree limbs. Our tallest guy is 5'9". Number 23 stretched on the sideline and listened to his coach as he studied us.

Coach Baldwin had told us not to worry about him, that he was going to get his points and rebounds, but if we could contain the rest of the team we had a good chance. Coach kept reminding us, "When he shoots, passes, breathes, whatever, get a hand in his face so he can't see."

They turned off the scoreboard toward the end of the game before us, and finally the slaughter was over. We took the floor and started our warm-ups.

"Goin' down, Red Rock," #23 said as he brushed past Duncan Swift and me. "Again."

CHAPTER 37

❀ Ashley ❀

I couldn't get back to sleep. I slogged downstairs and found Mom organizing the pantry. I could tell she was between book-writing projects, because that's always when she cleans or organizes.

"Hungry?" Mom said. I shrugged. "Feel like going to the Toot Toot?"

"Ready in five minutes," I said.

The Toot Toot Café sits next to the train tracks that run through Red Rock. It's owned by a sweet old couple, Bob and Helen Crumpus, who open early and serve breakfast all day. There's a counter with round stools at the front. You can get thick milk shakes and malts in metal shakers. Pieces of pie sit in a glass container. Helen squeezes fresh lemonade every day, and they have specials like meat loaf, fish, and all-you-can-eat pancakes. There are pictures on the wall, signed in tribute to the Toot Toot, of local people, mayors, teachers, and even sports stars.

High school kids work as waiters and waitresses, and when Mr. Crumpus heard about our dad dying in a plane crash, he said Bryce and I could work there in a couple of years.

"Guess you heard the attack happened right out back," the waitress said. "The guy used to sit in front. Mr. Crumpus gave him food." She leaned close. "I told Bob something like this was going to happen, but he wouldn't listen. I think he liked the guy."

"Really?"

She knelt and put her elbows on the table. "I was working the day the police called. Bob went outside and talked to him. By the time the police got here, he was gone."

CHAPTER 38

Bryce

I grabbed the tip-off, drove to the basket, and went in for the layup. I heard someone behind me, and as I planted my foot, the ball flew out of my hands and someone crashed into me. We both hit the floor. I looked back at the referee. "No foul?"

Duncan Swift was on the floor beside me. My own teammate had fouled me. "You were about to give them two points," he said, jumping up and holding out a hand.

I had raced for the wrong basket.

"Thanks."

Parents snickered on both sides of the gym. I tried not to look as we set up our defense.

"Shake it off," Coach Baldwin said.

The ball came in to #23 and I fouled him. He glared at me.

Coach Baldwin called me over while #23 sank both free throws. "Don't worry about that. Focus."

I nodded, trying to catch my breath.

Coach slapped me on the back. "It was a good shot. Good form." He smiled. "Just wait until the second half to shoot at that end."

I saw Sam in the stands. He was on the phone, but he gave me a thumbs-up. Why was he always on the phone?

At the half #23 had scored 15 points, but we were only four points down. The sleepover must've taken a lot out of me. I had only two points.

CHAPTER 39

❀ Ashley ❀

I chose the Belgian waffle with hot maple syrup. Half of it filled me up, so I packed the rest in a Styrofoam box. While Mom paid, I found Mr. Crumpus sweeping the front porch. His face was round and almost as red as the ketchup splotches on his white apron. He had combed over a wisp of hair from the left side to the right to cover a bald spot. I sat in a rocker and said hello.

"Have a good lunch?" he said.

I patted my full stomach. "As usual. Sounds like it's been pretty exciting around here."

He propped his broom against the railing and sat beside me. His face turned grim, as if he'd just eaten a rotten egg. "It's a sorry business."

"Does that guy live around here?" I said.

He pointed to a mountain peak. "Up there. The police have been looking for him."

"You don't think he's guilty?"

Mr. Crumpus stared at me. "Never say never. That's what I always say. That young man has had his share of trouble. The accident was the start."

"Accident?"

Mr. Crumpus waved a hand. "Long time ago. I never thought he could attack anyone."

"Running off makes him look guilty."

Mr. Crumpus shrugged. "Maybe he knew they wouldn't believe him. All I know is, that boy would never hurt anyone. Would I let someone stay around and feed him from my own grill if he'd hurt children?" He sighed. "I'm sorry. I get worked up about it, but I'm afraid for him. He was so close to turning around."

"What do you mean?"

"We'd talked about him working for me. Maybe going to church with Helen and me. Moving back home."

Mom came out, tucking her credit card in her purse. "What's up?"

Mr. Crumpus stood. "I was just telling her about Danny—the one . . ." He looked like he was in another world.

"I've been praying for him," Mom said.

CHAPTER 40

◉ *Bryce* ◉

Funny what you focus on while you're on the bench. Everybody figures you're champing at the bit to get back in, but I was playing so bad I hoped Coach Baldwin would leave me out. I was thinking about Sam. How could anyone marry the wife of a guy he had killed?

"Timberline, you're in!"

I ran to the scorer's table, checked in, and looked at the clock—2:03 remaining. It was 35–33, Coronado. Number 23 was shooting two free throws. He made the first but missed the second. Duncan got the rebound and threw an outlet pass to me.

"Push it up!" Coach yelled. "Go to the middle!"

I sliced between two defenders and headed for the basket. At the foul line, one of their players slapped at the ball and it hit my knee and bounced away. I could only watch, hoping one of their players wouldn't pick it up and go for a layup at the other end.

Out of nowhere Duncan shot to the sideline and grabbed it just before it went out-of-bounds. He looked over his shoulder, falling out-of-bounds, and tossed it to me right before his feet touched. Three players, including #23, swarmed. I pivoted left but couldn't find an open man. The ref was about to call five seconds on me when Duncan whistled. I rolled the ball through #23's legs straight to my teammate. All alone, he stepped to the three-point arc and fired a long shot. The swish of the net was the best thing I had heard since little Wally's giggle the night before. The ref put both hands in the air. We were tied at 36.

Mr. Swift went wild, flailing his clipboard and hollering, "Yes! Yes!"

We got back into our zone defense quickly and tried to keep the ball from #23. With 33 seconds left, their point guard shoved a bounce pass toward the big guy and he gathered it in. He faked left, turned right, and hit a layup.

"That's okay," Coach said during a time-out. "We have 30 seconds to get off a good shot. You've fought them tough all the way. Let's finish well." He diagrammed a play I had seen a hundred times. Duncan throws to the open man, then goes straight to the basket where he takes a pass and lays it in. Nine times out of 10, the defense forgets about him and Duncan has an easy layup.

I fought my way through a screen and got open. Duncan threw me the ball and went for the basket. Number 23 came out and blocked the passing lane. Duncan waved at me, but it was too late. A defender picked him up.

Before I could pass, #23 knocked the ball out of my hands. It slammed to the floor and bounced high, heading out-of-bounds. But #23 jumped, grabbed the ball, and threw it at me. Hard. I tried to duck, but the ball bonked off my face and out-of-bounds.

Their ball.

Only 22 seconds left.

And there was blood on the court.

Mine.

My eyes watered, and I saw little white things swimming in front of me. Someone handed me a towel, helped me up, and walked me back to the bench. I could tell by the boots that it was Sam. The parents clapped, but Mr. Swift was yelling at the refs.

One of the moms gave me an ice pack for my nose. My teammates patted me on the back. If I hadn't felt like I had a basketball growing out of my nose, I would have enjoyed the attention.

Coronado hit two more foul shots and won 40–36. We all lined up to slap hands and say, "Good game." I was the last player in our line, and #23 was the last in theirs.

He stopped and shook his head. "Hey, man, sorry. I was trying to bounce it off your leg, not your face." His voice was high, even higher than mine. He put a hand on my shoulder. "No hard feelings?"

I shook my head. "Ith all righ" was all I could manage.

CHAPTER 41

❀ Ashley ❀

Bryce's nose looked like a red cucumber. A faint backward imprint of the word *Spalding* ran across his forehead. I was sorry I'd missed the game. I like to be there for Bryce, but I love watching Duncan Swift. Not that I have a thing for him or anything. I just think he's good. Well, maybe I like him a little, but he doesn't know I exist.

Bryce went to his room with an ice pack. Dylan asked for his own, so I put ice cubes in a plastic bag for him. He came to Bryce's room holding the ice bag and pressing three Band-Aids on his nose.

Bryce smiled, then winced.

When we were alone, I told him what Mr. Crumpus had told me about the guy who attacked Tracy and Cammy.

Bryce sat up."What are you thinking?"

"I don't know. It's something about their story."

"You're just ticked about what Cammy said to you in the bathroom."

I shook my head. "It's more than that. Mr. Crumpus said something about an accident. Maybe we can find out more from Danny's parents."

"How are you going to get to them?"

"The fund-raiser for the dance studio. We're selling candles. If I can talk Mom into letting us go over there tomorrow on our ATVs, will you go?"

Bryce lifted the ice bag. "I'm there. I can use my nose as a headlight."

I found Mom in the kitchen, but before I could bring up the ATVs, she asked if I would go to the freezer in the barn and get two pizzas. I discovered the freezer strangely empty. There was only one bag of frozen corn.

"I bought four pizzas last week," Mom said. "Are you sure you looked carefully?"

I nodded. "But I can check again."

"No, that's okay. You look like you want to ask me something."

CHAPTER 42

Bryce

Jeff's mom offered to get me some ice for my nose, but my face already felt like a cherry snow cone. I put my sleeping bag and pillow down in their entryway.

Mrs. Alexander put a hand on my shoulder. "I don't think Jeff is up to a sleepover as it turns out, but he wants you to stay for a while. I can take you home later, after dark."

I found Jeff in his bedroom, looking through photos of people on bikes. He seemed tired, with circles under his eyes. He called me Rudolph the rest of the night and smiled weakly.

He closed the door and sat on his bed. "I can't talk to everybody about this, Timberline, but I figure you can handle it."

"Why?"

"Because of what happened to your dad. Lots of Christians give me all the verses they've memorized and tell me God's good. I know he is, but that didn't make my chemo any less painful."

I sat in a beanbag chair and looked at my hands. "I don't like it when you talk like this."

He cocked his head. "We're all gonna die, Bryce. Some a little faster than others, but we've all got to go through it."

He handed me a quote from some comedian. It read, "It's not that I'm afraid to die. I just don't want to be there when it happens."

I had to laugh. "So what are you thinking?" I said.

He pointed to the bicycle pictures. "There's this race, actually more of an endurance test. All the money they raise goes for cancer research."

The pictures showed people in colorful uniforms biking up hills, rock formations, and lonely trails. Some were riding because family members had died. Others just wanted to lend their support.

"It's something I want to do this summer if I'm strong enough."

He was having a hard time talking, let alone biking all those miles.

"I know I can't do it by myself, and my dad can't go because of his back problems. So I asked my parents if you and I could go together." A fire lit in his eyes, and he leaned closer. "There's this special bike two people can ride."

"A tandem."

"Yeah. They can fit it with oxygen or whatever we need. Would you go with me? You get to camp out at night by the trail. My parents would drive the minivan, and we could sleep in there."

"Why me?" I said.

"It's something we can look back on and laugh about. Plus, the more time you spend with a person, the better you get to know them. I figure if I go to heaven before you do, I could see your dad and tell him all the stuff you've been doing."

I looked at the pictures again, at the smiling kids with pasty white skin. They looked really alive. I thought about Sam. I'd been spending more time with him, but I still felt like I didn't know him at all.

"You won't even need a tandem," I said. "You'd beat me by a couple of miles."

Mrs. Alexander drove me home, and the more I thought about the bike trip, the better I liked the idea. It would give Jeff something to look forward to. I hoped he wouldn't wind up being too weak to go.

CHAPTER 43

❀ Ashley ❀

I asked Mom to break the drive rule for our ATVs, and to my surprise, she said Bryce and I could go out the next day. I felt like I had won a gold medal in Four-Wheeler Begging. She said we had to go during daylight hours, and I said that was fine.

Leigh came in with Randy and offered to take me out for ice cream. I'm not one to turn down free food, so I hurried outside before Leigh changed her mind.

"Are you scared to go out with that kook still on the loose?" Randy said on the way to his truck.

I shrugged.

Leigh took Randy's arm. "Big, strong football player like you can protect us, right?"

He rolled his eyes. "But what if the big, strong football player's not around when the guy shows up?"

"You think he's still around?" I said.

"One of my friends said the cops chased him this direction. He could be hiding out in your barn."

Leigh slugged him on the shoulder, then looked behind her.

CHAPTER 44

☺ *Bryce* ☺

I couldn't believe it when Ashley said we could ride the ATVs after church. It had been almost a week since we had ridden them to school, the longest we had ever gone.

Ashley had her candle catalog, and we stopped at Mrs. Watson's house first, where we park every school day. Sam had known Mrs. Watson for a long time, and she usually bought something from us.

As the woman flipped through the catalog, Ashley asked if she knew anything about the Ingram family.

"That man who hurt the girls?" Mrs. Watson said, her rocking chair going. She held the catalog to her chest and squinted out the window. "The family moved into that fortress yonder a few years ago. Can't get in or out without going through a big old fence. Secretive bunch, I've heard. Don't talk much."

I leaned forward and put my hands on my knees. "How long have you known Sam?"

"Ever since he bought your place. I think he has a thing for me." She winked and fluffed her white hair. "Your mother is a looker, but I think Sam prefers a little age."

"Come on, Mrs. Watson. What do you know about him?"

Her rocker stopped. "I worried about him when he moved in with that little girl of his, all alone. I offered to cook for him. I was glad when he found your mother and you birds moved in."

"But what about his past? What did he do before?"

"Some kind of military, I suppose," she said. "A lot of pilots around here are former air force. Why don't you ask *him*?"

CHAPTER 45

❀ Ashley ❀

Bryce beat me to the Ingrams' driveway and turned off his ATV. There aren't many houses in this part of Red Rock—if this is even part of Red Rock. From here you're so close to the mountain that you can't see Pikes Peak. Funny how something smaller can block out something bigger when you're close.

We slipped off our helmets, and Bryce studied the property. The house was at the end of a long driveway that snaked up the hill to a plateau covered with pine trees. To the left stood a corral with a small barn. Huge timbers rose out of the ground and arched over the driveway. A barbed-wire fence ran along the road and directly up the hill to a closed gate. A small keypad was fixed to the middle, and another square box with a button was attached to the timber.

"You don't think he could be hiding here, do you?" Bryce said.

"The police would have searched it."

Bryce climbed off his ATV and placed his helmet on the seat. "Do you like this as much as I do?"

"What?"

"Snooping around. Trying to solve a mystery."

I nodded. "Except . . ."

"What?"

"I'd rather not be part of the mystery about Sam and Dad."

Bryce told me what he had overheard on the answering machine and what he had learned from his Internet search.

"Is that why you grilled Mrs. Watson?" I said.

He nodded. "Think about it, Ash. We don't know anything about Sam's parents other than the pictures he shows us. We don't know what he did before Mom met him, other than fly famous people around. For all we know, he could be mixed up with those gold robbers or—"

"A spy for the government?" I said.

"Anything."

"You kids get out of here!" someone shouted from the hillside. "Can't you read?"

CHAPTER 46

☺ *Bryce* ☺

Ashley slapped her hand over her mouth as a guy walked toward us, carrying some kind of tool. He looked older, maybe in his 50s, with stubbly gray whiskers, and he wore a wide hat pulled down to his eyebrows.

"Sign says No Trespassing. Get out of here."

I grabbed my helmet and slammed it on, but Ashley walked toward the fence holding out her catalog. "My name's Ashley Timberline, and I go to the Peak Academy of Dance. We're having a fund-raiser with these candles. I'm sure your wife would love one."

The guy's eyes softened, and it almost looked like he was going to smile. "No, we don't need any candles."

"What about your wife? Do you think I could talk to her?"

He walked toward us slowly, like from a dock onto an unsteady rowboat. "Timberline. You Sam's kids?"

"Yes, we are. This is my brother Bryce."

He stared at me. "What happened to you?"

I told him about the basketball game, and this time he did smile.

"You know Sam?" Ashley said.

He nodded. "Flew some friends and me to Montana once. See him every now and then around town."

A car approached and the man reached through the fence. "Harriet's not here right now. Let me see your candles, and you can pick this up tomorrow after school."

CHAPTER 47

❀ Ashley ❀

Mom was watching for us as we neared our house. Bryce and I were excited about making contact with the Ingrams, but we didn't tell Mom or Sam.

Leigh hopped into the house announcing that she was going to ace her driver's test. Randy had told her she was as good a driver as he was, but he has more dents in his truck than I have old Beanie Babies. Still, I hoped she would pass.

When I brought up driving the ATVs after school, Mom said she and Sam wanted us to wait.

"But you let us go today," I said.

"That's our decision," Mom said.

I was tempted to go on a hunger strike, but Mom made her taco casserole, which I thought cruel and unusual because I can't pass it up. After dinner, Bryce and I went out on the back porch and ate orange Push-Ups.

"How are we gonna get back to the Ingrams' house?" Bryce said.

"We'll get Mom to drive us or we'll walk," I said.

The stars were starting to appear. I noticed a strange glow coming from the red rocks behind our house. I pointed it out to Bryce, but he didn't see it.

CHAPTER 48

⊙ *Bryce* ⊙

"Come straight home on the bus," Mom said the next morning.

Ashley bristled.

"But Ash has more houses to take her catalog to," I said. "And we left one at this lady's place. I bet she'll buy a whole page."

Mom sighed. "Sam and I agree it's not a good idea for you guys to be out alone. Dylan has a doctor's appointment later or I'd take you."

"Can we walk?" Ashley said.

Mom shook her head. "It'll have to wait until I get home."

"But, Mom—," Ashley started.

"Bus!" Dylan shouted.

At school I saw Cammy and Tracy talking to a group. When Cammy saw us she whispered something. Ashley walked past without a word.

Back home that afternoon I looked for the Ingrams' phone number on the Internet and in the phone book. No luck. Then I went into the database of *The Gazette* from Colorado Springs and searched for any story with Danny Ingram in it. I came up empty.

By the time Mom got back, she had to get dinner started. She said we could go candle selling later, but after a few phone calls and word that Sam would be late, it was almost dark. Ashley brooded like a wounded animal, but it didn't do any good.

Tuesday afternoon Mom drove us into town. We didn't want her to know we had gone as far as the Ingram house, but there was no denying it. "If I'd have known you were coming this far," she said, "I'd never have agreed."

She waited in the car while Ashley and I walked to the gate. The catalog was sticking out of the newspaper box. Ashley opened it quickly and looked at the order form. It was partially filled out with their name and phone number, but nothing was checked to order.

I pushed the Intercom button, but there was no answer.

A police cruiser drove by, kicking up dust.

CHAPTER 49

❀ Ashley ❀

After pestering Sam and Mom for another whole day, Bryce and I got them to let us ride our ATVs to school Thursday morning. I heard the beep of Bryce's digital watch, and we had our cereal and were out the door before Mom could ask why we were leaving so early.

We rode as fast as we dared and cut across the grassland between us and the dirt road that leads to the Ingrams'. The rock formation loomed behind us like a red ghost. Bryce kept checking his watch.

When we rounded the corner and came near the Ingrams' driveway, the gate stood wide open. We stopped and took off our helmets. "What do you think?" I said.

"It'll take us 10 minutes to get to Mrs. Watson's and another five to make it into school. We have only about 10 minutes to spare."

"Good, let's go."

Bryce shrugged and followed me up the driveway. A black-and-brown dog with only three legs met us. The thing didn't bark. It just wagged its tail and hopped close enough to sniff us.

We parked by the garage and waited. When no one came out, I walked the gravel path around to the front door and knocked.

"Mom will be ticked if she finds out," Bryce said.

Before I could answer, the door opened and an older woman stared at us. She had puffy eyes and shiny skin and looked like one of those people you see in ads for retirement homes—the people with a golf club in one hand and a glass of tea in the other—except she wasn't smiling. "How did you get in?"

"The gate was open," I said.

She ran a hand through her hair. "Walter is meeting with a reporter. He must have forgotten to close it."

I explained who we were and pulled the catalog out of my backpack. "I don't know if your husband showed you this."

She looked at Bryce, then back at me. "Shouldn't you be in school?"

"That's where we're headed. We only have a minute. May we come in?"

The house was full of furniture, yet it looked empty. An old wedding picture hung on the living-room wall. Another picture showed a young man with a football on his knee and a helmet under his arm. "Who's that?"

"That's our Danny," she said, sighing. "I suppose you've heard about him."

We walked to the kitchen, and I pulled out a chair. Bryce stood in the hall looking at his watch.

"The police haven't found him yet?" I said.

She took the catalog and flipped through the pages. "I wish they would. I'm scared of what might happen if they don't. Danny has done some bad things, but he'd never hurt anyone."

Were these people blind, or could that be true?

CHAPTER 50

Bryce

The big clock in the hallway ticked like a time bomb, and I knew we'd be in trouble if we were late. The school would call home and we'd have to explain. I was about to signal to Ashley that we had to go when Mrs. Ingram closed the catalog.

"You don't have to buy anything," Ashley said. "We know how hard this must be."

"The police think we're hiding Danny, but I haven't seen him in two weeks."

"Why did he leave?" Ashley said.

"We tried to get him to come back, but he wouldn't. I don't think he could forgive himself."

"For what?"

"There was an accident."

"Ashley, we should go," I said.

She looked at me like I had just taken another leg off the dog. "What accident? Around here?"

She shook her head. "Before we moved. It was early one morning when Danny was still in college. He had gotten a summer job at a golf course near our home. He saw a dog by the road."

"The one outside?"

She nodded. "Danny felt sorry for the poor thing. He was going to give it something to eat at the clubhouse and bring it home that night. But something happened. It was awful."

I looked at my watch again, but there was no way I was leaving now.

"Rex, the dog, got up on the front seat and got sick. Danny tried to move him onto the floor, but he wouldn't budge. Then it happened. Danny hit something on the side of the road. He thought it was an animal, but when he stopped and walked back, he found a man in the weeds."

"Oh no," Ashley said.

"We knew him and his family. He was a great father. Three little children. Danny ran to the nearest house and called an ambulance, but the man died on the way to the hospital."

"How awful."

"Danny felt terrible. The police talked about charges, but everybody knew it was an accident. Everybody but Danny. He dropped out of school and never went back to the golf course. Fell in with a bad crowd and started drinking. We moved here to make a fresh start, but Danny just couldn't get over it. He left the house about a year ago and started living on the street. Every now and then we'd hear he was back in Red Rock, and we'd try to get him to come home."

"Mr. Crumpus says nice things about him," Ashley said.

"Bob Crumpus is one of the bright spots in our lives. I've always thought the Lord could change my son, but I don't think he hears my prayers anymore."

Ashley put a hand on the woman's arm. "Where do you think Danny might have gone? Bryce and I would like to help."

She stared at Ashley with red eyes. "I'd love to have Danny back, but even if you did find him, it's too late. Our son is gone for good."

CHAPTER 51

❀ Ashley ❀

We made it inside the school doors just as the first bell rang. I could see the relief on Bryce's face as we hurried to our lockers.

I thought about Danny the rest of the day. He must have felt so guilty. I remembered seeing him at the Toot Toot Café and thinking he was just a bum. I was ashamed I had judged him without knowing anything about him.

At lunch I took my tray across the cafeteria and sat near some of the eighth graders. Cammy and Tracy had their usual crowd of giggling girls. I caught only bits of the conversation.

". . . won't mess with us anymore . . ."

". . . lucky we took care of him when we did . . ."

". . . everybody knew he was dangerous . . ."

". . . catch him and bring him back here for the trial . . ."

". . . hope he stays gone for good."

Cammy looked at me, and I focused on my lunch. She kept staring until I looked up. "Hey, Timberline, what do *you* think they should do with the guy who attacked us?"

The other girls were suddenly quiet.

"Get his side of the story, for starters," I said.

"We know what happened," Cammy said. "We were there."

I nodded. "I guess you're right."

"So answer the question."

"Justice," I said.

I didn't look back, but from their silence, I assumed Cammy and Tracy weren't happy.

CHAPTER 52

Bryce

Sam drove me to basketball practice. I still had bruises around my eyes.

Coach Baldwin worked on fundamentals. That meant we ran a lot, passed a lot, and didn't shoot much. The tournament was coming, and he wanted us in shape. We had beaten every team we faced except for Coronado, so we felt good about our chances.

"It's tough to beat a team three times in the same year," Coach said. "I've got some strategy for that big guy."

"Use Bryce's head for defense," Duncan Swift said.

Everybody laughed, including me, but it hurt. Duncan's the kind of guy who competes at everything. Sports, math, even bathroom visits. After a Super-Mega Slushie, I once timed myself and told Duncan I had gone for 58 seconds. The next day he said he had gone a minute and 20 seconds after drinking 16 lemonades. I didn't believe him, but I vowed never to tell him anything concerning bodily functions again. I figured I might need a transplant if we kept it up.

As we got dressed, Riley Coleman, our biggest player, started talking about how cute Cammy and Tracy are.

"I hear Cammy's dad is mean as a snake," Duncan said.

"*Mean* isn't the word for it," Riley said. "And it's her stepdad. You know how they can be."

I shivered. Sam was our stepdad, and though he had never been mean to us, I had my questions.

"My sister says Cammy's mom is no better," Carlos said. "She yelled at my mom at the library."

"Tracy's mom's a yeller too," Riley said. "I saw her chew Tracy out in the Blockbuster parking lot. She threw a DVD at her."

I had to tell Ashley. As I walked outside I found Sam sitting on a rock. He was on the phone, facing the Front Range.

". . . I think I owe them that much, don't you?" Sam said forcefully. "Tim, I disagree. You've never been in my situation. How could you possibly know . . . ?"

I stopped and tried to listen, but Sam noticed me and lowered his voice. He clicked his phone shut. "How'd practice go?"

"Who was that?" I said.

Sam hesitated. "Just business."

CHAPTER 53

Ashley

Mom asked me to get some sweet corn from the freezer in the barn. Now *that* I knew we had.

But I was wrong. It was gone. And so was everything else.

I walked slowly back inside, staring at the red rocks behind our house. Sam had warned us not to climb them without the right gear, that the holes in the rocks made perfect places for animals. Bryce and I had driven around them, and we'd climbed a few feet, but we'd never *really* explored the rocks.

I opened the kitchen freezer and pulled out a dwindling bag of peas. "Mom, we must have used the corn already."

"You hate peas," she said.

She was right. "All I am saying is give peas a chance," I said.

She shook her head.

During dinner I asked if Bryce and I could take a quick ride out to the red rocks.

Sam looked at the setting sun. The days were getting longer and warmer. "For a few minutes," he said. "But be back by dark."

CHAPTER 54

Bryce

I had no idea what Ashley was up to, but I wasn't about to pass up a ride on the ATVs. About halfway to the rocks, she slowed and motioned for me to stop. "Something's going on out here. There's more stuff gone from the freezer, and remember the weird glow the other night?"

"Where?" Bryce said.

"Near the praying hands."

There's a formation of rocks that looks like two hands touching, with a V-shaped hole underneath. To me it looks more like two porcupines rubbing noses.

We had to slow when we reached a rocky area near the base of the formation. Small red stones dotted the landscape. If you run over one of them going fast you can flip.

Ashley veered right, stopped, and got off the Ashleymobile. I pulled close as she held up a piece of melted plastic. She pointed at a white swan near the top of the bag. "Our corn."

"Could have blown out of the trash," I said.

"Yeah, but how did it melt?" She stuffed the bag in her pocket.

We continued up to a plateau where we parked. The red rocks blocked our view of the house now, and the setting sun shone through the opening of the praying hands.

"Somebody's up in that big cave below the hands," Ashley said. "If there was a fire in there, it would glow up through the hands and we'd see it, don't you think?"

We jogged up the path to get a better view. The rocks are about as long as two football fields, and around the base are scrub oaks and wildflowers. We climbed, hopping from one rock to another.

Suddenly something screamed above us.

Ashley turned, white-faced. "Mountain lion!"

CHAPTER 55

✾ Ashley ✾

As we flew down toward our vehicles, I kept waiting for the wildcat to jump on our backs and drag one of us away. On the local news I'd seen stories about mountain lions attacking dogs in backyards. Kids had been picked off while walking ahead of their parents on remote trails.

People tell mountain lion tales all the time. At a retreat near Colorado Springs a few years ago women were outside, sipping tea, watching a flock of bighorn sheep graze on the hillside. Suddenly, one of the women screamed as a mountain lion jumped one of the sheep and tore it apart. Blood everywhere. The women ran inside while the mountain lion had his own tea and cookies.

Mom and I hate that story, but Bryce tells it as often as he can, and he always exaggerates the bloody part.

Mountain lion attacks usually happen in the summer, and since it was still spring, Bryce and I should have been safe, but we weren't taking any chances.

We jumped on our ATVs and raced away, careful of rocks and ruts. Halfway home I stopped.

Bryce pulled up beside me. "Scary, huh?"

I nodded, trying to catch my breath. "I'd hate to have to go home and tell them a cougar ate you."

Bryce pointed to his face. "I look like a bruised banana. He would have taken one look at you and pounced." He looked back. "What are we going to do about our helmets?"

I hadn't even noticed we'd left them. "We can go back tomorrow," I said. "Those things don't feed early in the day."

"They feed when they're hungry," Bryce said.

CHAPTER 56

☺ *Bryce* ☺

That night I stayed up late looking for the glow Ashley talked about. I saw nothing but starry skies and heard only the occasional cry of baby coyotes. I dreamed of a monster wildcat attacking us with teeth as big as my hand. Ashley and I were running toward the house when the cat veered off and went for Dylan.

That's all I can remember, but when I woke up I had to go to Dylan's room and make sure he was okay. He sleeps with his mouth open, so it sounds like Thomas the Tank Engine pulling into the station.

After breakfast the next morning, Ashley occupied Mom and I

stole outside to the barn. I pushed the ATV outside to the back so it wouldn't make too much noise. Just before I turned the key, I heard someone behind me.

"See anything last night?" Sam said, a coffee cup in his hands.

"Not really," I said. *We didn't see anything. We simply heard a cougar scream.*

"Going back for your helmets?" Sam said.

I nodded. *Was he spying on us?* Sam always seemed to know a lot more than we thought.

"Be careful."

The cool air felt good in my hair as I sped along. The biggest adventure most kids have before school is brushing their teeth, but I was going into the teeth of mountain lion country.

I slowed when I came to the back of the rock formation, looking carefully right and left. We'd left the helmets on the plateau. I swallowed hard, then accelerated to the path. Something sparkling in the golden sunlight caught my eye. There's nothing like a Colorado sunrise.

I drove left and couldn't believe my eyes.

Our helmets.

Someone had placed them on the rocks.

CHAPTER 57

❀ Ashley ❀

Things weren't going well with my candle sales—other than Mom and Mrs. Watson, they were zilch—but I had a lot on my mind. We had tests coming up in math and English, but with a dance lesson the next day, I had to do more selling.

Mom said I could go after school, but only if Bryce went with me.

We drove our ATVs across the railroad tracks to my friend Hayley's, where I was sure her mom would buy something. But Hayley's mom wasn't home.

"Try Cammy's house," Hayley said, smirking and pointing down the street.

I looked at Bryce. "Maybe we will."

We left our ATVs and walked up the street. Cammy's house is older than most around it. The roof looked like it was falling apart. Most of the front yard was small rocks. Scraggly bushes poked through weeds and cedar chips. Brown patches of grass spread around the edges of the house. Old newspapers lay in the driveway, turning yellow from the sun.

"What are you doing?" Bryce said.

"Seeing if we can talk with Cammy's mom," I said, smiling. "Maybe she'll buy a candle."

The doorbell had wires sticking out of it, so I knocked and took a step back. A dog barked and someone shouted at it.

Finally, Mrs. Michaels came to the door with a cigarette in one hand and a phone in the other. Her wet hair dripped onto her robe. "Thought you were Cammy," she said. "Can I help you?"

I held out the catalog.

"I've got somebody at the door," she said into the phone.

I pointed to several inexpensive candles on the back cover.

"Wish I could help you, but I'm getting ready for work, and anyway, I really can't afford anything."

I took the catalog back. "It's okay. I was thinking you might buy one for Cammy, you know, to cheer her up."

"She'd probably burn the house down," Mrs. Michaels said, sneering. "You seen her? She's supposed to watch her brother so I can go to work."

I shook my head. "We go to school with her. We heard what happened."

She rolled her eyes. "You and everybody in town. I told her if she made me late for work one more time I was going to—"

A group of kids approached, Cammy in the middle, puffing a cigarette.

Her mother yelled at her, then closed the door.

Bryce and I walked down the cracked driveway and skirted the group.

Cammy glared at me. “What are you doing here?”

We didn’t answer.

CHAPTER 58

Bryce

After Ashley and I got home from not selling candles, I went to the barn before dinner. When I got to the top of the stairs, I went into Sam's office. I knew it was wrong to snoop, but I was dying for more information about him.

Mail littered the top of his desk, but it looked like just a bunch of bills. I opened the desk drawer and found files listed: Invoices, Insurance, Tax docs, Utilities, Car repair, S-Corp Current.

Then I came to a file that simply said Letters. I pulled it from the drawer and sat in Sam's leather chair. The letter on the top was on official letterhead from Washington D.C. I flipped through and found more letters from the same office.

One was addressed to Sam Timberline at our address. The date showed it was before we moved to Colorado.

> Dear Mr. Timberline,
>
> I am pleased to hear that you have settled into your new home. I trust things are going well in this difficult transition. Rest assured many here are aware of the sacrifice you have made for your country.
>
> If there is anything we can do for you and your daughter, please don't hesitate to ask. I'm hoping one day you'll be able to return to Washington when we apprehend the perpetrators of this heinous crime.
>
> Godspeed and success in your new business. Maybe one of these days you can fly my family and me to one of the ski resorts out there.

It was signed by the director of the Department of Homeland Security. I felt guilty about going through Sam's stuff, so I put the letter back in the file and tried to return it to the drawer. But the file was too full. I rearranged the letters and pulled the drawer out all the way. It slipped off its rollers and thudded to the floor.

I knelt, pushed the file in, then tried to get the drawer back onto its rollers. Something caught my eye at the back of the desk—a smushed envelope wedged in the corner. I grabbed it.

The postmark was smudged so I couldn't read the date, but it looked pretty old. The return address said it was from Marshall Faulkner somewhere in Germany. It was addressed to Lynn Vickers.

A door banged downstairs and my heart jumped. *Sam's not supposed to be back yet!*

I picked up the drawer, got it back on track, and shoved it closed. I stashed the letter in my pocket and tiptoed to the exercise room.

CHAPTER 59

❀ Ashley ❀

Mom showed me two articles in the newspaper after dinner. The first included an interview with Tracy and Cammy. The headline read, "Local Girls Talk about Safety."

The article began:

> Cammy Michaels, 14, and Tracy Elliot, 13, know what it's like to be scared. Since last week's alleged assault in Red Rock, the girls have used their terrifying experience to teach younger children about protecting themselves.
>
> Tracy said in an interview from her home, "When they

hear about us getting tied up and threatened, their eyes go wide and some of them start to cry. We want them to imagine what it was like so it won't happen to them."

The article went on to name the suspect.

"We still have the tape he used to remind us of what happened," Cammy said. "I'll never forget that day."

I took the whole section to my room to read. Something bothered me, and not just because Cammy had been so mean to me. Something was not right.

An inside page carried an interview with Mr. Ingram and a picture of him. He held a picture of his son and looked sad.

There was nothing in the story about Danny's accident, but it did call him "troubled."

The reporter asked Mr. Ingram if he believed his son had hurt the two girls.

"I can't imagine that, but I have to believe their story," Mr. Ingram said. "But if you knew my son a few years ago, if you would have seen how hard he worked and how kind he was, you wouldn't believe he could do this. He was a wonderful student. He was creative and enjoyed sports. He climbed mountains and once won a contest for imitating animal calls. I just hope we get him home before something happens to him."

CHAPTER 60

Bryce

After dinner I went to my room and closed the door. The letter felt like a nuclear bomb. I was afraid Sam would empty my pockets and say he knew I was going through his stuff. He seemed to know everything.

The brown envelope smelled musty. A weird stamp in the corner had foreign writing—it must have been German. I didn't know Lynn Vickers or Marshall Faulkner, so I wondered if Sam had bought the desk used and the letter wasn't even his.

I opened the letter carefully and pulled out a card. On the outside was a picture of a cute puppy with its head low to the ground. Beside him was somebody holding a gun.

The card read, "Have a happy birthday or I shoot the dog."

I laughed. Then I read the note inside.

Dear Lynn,

Just sitting here thinking of you and how much I wish I could be there to help you celebrate. I'm X-ing the days off my calendar for when I return stateside.

I still can't believe we're getting married. That you would have me as your husband makes me the happiest man in the world. I hope you haven't had second thoughts. :)

Training is almost over and I can't wait to see you. I carry your picture with me every minute of the day. (The other guys are jealous when they see it, by the way.)

I'll toast you on the morning of your birthday.

All my love,
Marshall

I put the card back in the envelope and slipped it into my pocket. The writing looked like Sam's. Could Marshall be his nickname? Or was it someone else? And who was Lynn?

Worse, what if Mom found out about this?

CHAPTER 61

❀ Ashley ❀

After helping Mom get Dylan to bed—he was wearing one of Leigh's hats and Bryce's basketball shorts—I went back to my room. The full moon shone on the red rocks, looking creepy and beautiful at the same time.

I opened my diary, lit my candle, and pulled out my Bible. I try to have devotions at least once a day, reading from the Bible and writing my thoughts. Mom had given me a book of thoughts by a Christian singer, but I couldn't relate to a lot of it. The singer talked about "trials" and "disappointments," but when I read closer it was more about a dog that had surgery or a house addition that took too long. When your dad is killed in a plane crash, that's a real trial.

I glanced out the window and noticed something moving in the barn.

A lone figure stepped out, closed the door, then started running toward the rocks.

CHAPTER 62

Bryce

Ashley burst into my room and grabbed my arm. "Come on."

I followed as she raced downstairs.

Mom stuck her head out of her office and asked where we were going.

"Showing Bryce something," Ashley said, then banged out the kitchen door.

She ran toward the barn, and it took me a few seconds to catch up. "I don't think he did it," she said.

"Who did what?"

"Danny. I don't think he attacked Tracy and Cammy."

"They're lying?"

She ran into the barn and hopped on the Ashleymobile. "Follow me."

CHAPTER 63

✾ Ashley ✾

I roared out of the barn, Bryce right behind me. We usually don't drive much after dark, especially on the bumpy land behind us, but this was the only way we'd catch up with the guy. All the stuff missing from the freezer and Sam's fridge—it made sense now.

We drove almost all the way to the rocks before I stopped. Wind whistled around us, and I had to shield my face from the dust and sand.

"What in the world—?" Bryce started.

I held up a hand and told him what I had seen and read. "I think the guy's holed up out here."

"What if you're wrong?" Bryce said. "It could have been Sam. Or one of those gold robbers. Or a real mountain lion."

I had a sick feeling. What if the guy was waiting to jump us?

CHAPTER 64

Bryce

I was excited about trying to find the intruder. But Ashley decided we should go home and call the police. We were headed back when something caught my eye. I saw a flash of white, then nothing. I slowed and pointed my ATV into the darkness.

Nothing.

A few minutes later we were back in the barn. We couldn't find anything missing, but Ashley went to the freezer. Mom had stocked it the day before. Now it was empty.

"That's it," I said. "Call the police."

"Wait," Ashley said. "If this is Danny, he must be scared out of his mind. He's just trying to survive."

"The guy is wanted by the police!"

"But I don't think he attacked those girls. And no one's going to believe him. They'll believe—" Ashley stopped and her eyes widened.

I turned to see Sam, his hands on his hips. "What's going on?" he said.

Ashley gushed the story.

Sam ran upstairs to his office, taking the steps three at a time. We found him rummaging through a closet. He pulled a weird-looking telescope from a box and went to the back window.

"What's that?" I said.

"Night-vision scope."

Where did he get that?

He stared into the distance, then handed the scope to Ashley. He pointed at the rocks and she gasped.

"What?" I said.

She passed me the scope, and I aimed it out the window. I couldn't keep my hands steady at first. Then Sam pulled my left hand farther out on the scope, and it was easier.

I could see like it was almost day, with a strange green tint to everything. A man walked across a ridge on the rocks.

Sam picked up the phone.

"Wait," Ashley said. "I need to tell you something before you call the police."

I still had the scope pointed at the guy. He was holding his arms out. Then suddenly they flew over his head. He lost his balance and fell out of sight.

CHAPTER 65

❀ Ashley ❀

I told Sam what I thought had happened to the food in the freezer and that I didn't think Danny had actually hurt Cammy and Tracy.

He didn't ask me why. He just glanced at me funny, threw the phone on his leather chair, and raced down the stairs. He hopped in his four-wheel-drive truck, and Bryce and I jumped in beside him.

When I told Sam about the mountain lion's scream his mouth dropped open. "You came out here again, even though you heard a cougar last night?"

We bounced along. Bryce said, "Why would that guy be climbing on this side of the rocks if he's staying in that big cave up there?"

"Most people don't know it," Sam said, "but a ridge runs along this side that leads through the praying hands to the other side. If he's climbed here, he probably knows that."

Sam grabbed a flashlight from the glove compartment, and we got out. Afraid we'd find Danny's body, I hung back.

A coyote yelped, and baby coyotes yipped in answer. They almost sounded human.

Were they warning us?

CHAPTER 66

Bryce

I kept up with Sam while Ashley lagged behind. The moon slipped behind a cloud, but the night was clear.

"Danny!" Sam called. "Can you hear us?"

A train whistle blew in the distance. Cars sped by on I-25, their headlights like orderly fireflies. Funny what you think of when you're looking for somebody who's dead.

We stayed with Sam and moved up the ledge. He climbed like a gymnast, like he could run along a balance beam without breaking stride. The ledge was easy at first, but then it got narrow and Sam told us to stay where we were.

But he has the flashlight.

Before I could protest, Ashley pointed. "What's that?"

Sam shined the light below and something moved.

"Hope it's not a real cougar," I whispered.

We heard short breaths and moaning, and Sam motioned us back off the ledge. He led us down a steep part of the rock to another path.

When we came around a huge rock, someone said, "Don't come any closer!"

CHAPTER 67

Ashley

Sam moved toward the big rock. All three of us looked around the edge. The man wore a green army jacket over a white shirt. His jeans were torn at the knee, and his hiking boots were dirty. They were so worn that he had duct taped them together.

Duct tape! Cammy and Tracy had said he used duct tape on them. Maybe this guy wasn't innocent after all.

"Danny?" Sam said.

His short beard made him look like a rock star. "Yeah."

"You hurt?" Sam said.

"Lost my footing." He tried to point but winced. "Landed funny on my arm, crawled over here."

"You been taking stuff from our barn?" Sam's voice didn't sound angry.

"Vegetables, some corn dogs, and a few pizzas. Those were a real bear to cook. I'm going to pay you back as soon as I get a job."

"People are looking for you," Sam said.

"Your parents," Bryce said.

Danny stared at the ground. "What are people saying?"

"That you hurt some girls," Sam said.

Danny shook his head. "I never touched anybody."

Sam pulled out his cell phone and dialed.

Danny tried to stand. "You're not taking me—" He fell back against the rock, holding his arm.

Sam identified himself and gave our address. "We have an injured climber on the red rocks and need an ambulance. And we need an officer too. We've found the guy you're looking for."

Sam hung up. "I want to call your family."

"I don't want them involved."

Sam dialed information, but I knew the number was unlisted. Then I remembered my candle order form.

Bryce and I ran toward the house, and Sam stayed with Danny. Bryce told Mom what was going on while I ran to my room and grabbed the order form. I dialed the Ingrams, and Danny's mother answered.

CHAPTER 68

☺ Bryce ☺

Ashley and I rode back to the rocks on our ATVs as the ambulance and police arrived. Sam sat on a rock a few feet from Danny, and we could tell they had been talking.

Ashley said, "I have to know. Did you make that cougar sound?"

Danny nodded. "Thought it would scare you off."

"Where'd you get the duct tape?" she said, pointing to his shoes.

Danny cocked his head. "Mr. Crumpus. Why?"

"Just wondering," Ashley said.

Sam helped Danny up. He wasn't as tall as I thought he'd be. His face was covered with freckles and he was skinny. This guy didn't seem like a monster at all.

Ashley and I followed Sam's truck back to the ambulance and police cruiser. Another car pulled in. Mr. Ingram.

Danny looked at Ashley when he got out of the truck. "Your dad says you think I'm not guilty. You're right, but no one will believe me."

"Your father will," Ashley said.

Danny pursed his lips. "Make those girls tell the truth."

CHAPTER 69

❀ Ashley ❀

I had to get to the truth. I was responsible for Danny being caught, and if he was innocent and still went to jail, I'd feel terrible.

Danny didn't speak to his father as he was led away.

Mr. Ingram thanked us for calling him and followed the police cars. The look on his face haunted me through the night and through church the next day. Everyone was talking about the capture.

Hayley called to find out what had happened, and I told her I couldn't get Danny's words out of my head.

"What are you going to do?" she said.

I thought about Tracy and Cammy. "I don't know, but as much as I hate being around those girls, I have to do something."

Bryce came into the room as soon as I hung up. "Whatever you need, I'll help," he said.

CHAPTER 70

◎ *Bryce* ◎

At school on Monday I switched my minirecorder on and slipped it into my shirt pocket. Then I met Ashley in the lunchroom. She had her brown bag and candle catalog out as she moved toward Tracy. Cammy was nowhere in sight. We heard she was making up an English test.

"Anybody here like candles?" Ashley said in a little-girl voice.

The girls looked at each other and rolled their eyes. Ashley went straight to Tracy and sat across from her. The others stared like Ash had leeches hanging from her.

"Tracy, whose idea was it to make up that story, yours or Cammy's?"

Tracy dropped her spoon in her chocolate pudding and it slopped on her. She tried to wipe it off with a napkin, but it smeared right into her pink shirt.

Ashley was using our mom's method of getting the truth. One day, instead of asking if we cut a tree down, she said, "I'll bet it was pretty hard to cut down that tree."

I spoke right up. "No, it wasn't that hard. Ashley bent it down a little and I . . ." I told her everything.

No such luck with Tracy. The pudding distracted her enough to give her time to think. With everyone at the table looking at her, she said, "We told the truth. That guy attacked us. Now the police caught him, and I'm glad."

"Even though he's innocent?" Ashley said.

A girl said, "You're taking up for that drunk?"

"How many more people does he have to attack before you believe us?" Tracy said.

Ashley pursed her lips.

Strike one against us.

CHAPTER 71

❀ Ashley ❀

Bryce and I moved to the hall outside Cammy's English classroom and ate. Every few minutes Bryce peeked inside.

"She's pulling at her hair," he said. "It's a wonder she's not bald."

Finally we heard Cammy's heels clacking on the floor, and Bryce clicked on his recorder. She wore a short skirt and carried a bright red purse over one shoulder. She looked really pretty.

"Hey, Cammy," I said as she closed the door behind her, "how'd your test go?"

She glanced our way as if we were termites and kept walking.

"We just talked with Tracy about the story you two made up."

Cammy stopped dead in her tracks and stared. She suddenly had that ugly stepsister look, like an animal backed into a corner. When she opened her mouth, I imagined I could see fangs. "What did she say?"

"That it was the truth," I said.

Cammy gritted her teeth and hurried down the hall.

Bryce switched off his recorder. "Strike two."

CHAPTER 72

☺ *Bryce* ☺

We left our ATVs at Mrs. Watson's and walked to town so Ashley could keep trying to sell candles. We stopped at the Toot Toot Café, where Mr. Crumpus was setting out silverware for the dinner rush.

He smiled. "Would you two get older so you can do this?"

"We'll be 14 soon," Ashley said. "If you count seven months soon."

Mr. Crumpus noticed Ashley's catalog. "The dance studio?"

"Don't tell me you've already bought something."

"Three things for the counter so far. Guess one more wouldn't hurt."

"You know they caught Danny last night behind our house," I said.

"Yeah," Mr. Crumpus said, writing on the sheet. "Guess I was wrong about him."

"What do you mean?" Ashley said.

"Haven't you heard? He confessed. Said he did it. A customer told me."

Ashley's face turned white. "But he told us . . ."

Mr. Crumpus excused himself to seat some customers.

"Strike three, Ash," I said. "Come on, let's go."

CHAPTER 73

❀ Ashley ❀

We walked right by the police station, where TV news vans were parked with tall antennas and satellite dishes pointed to the sky. I wanted to go in and ask if it was true. Could I have been wrong about Cammy and Tracy?

Bryce pecked me on the shoulder and motioned to the other side of the street. Cammy and Tracy hurried along, talking loudly. Bryce and I moved behind the corner of a building and watched.

Tracy turned and said something. Then Cammy grabbed her arm and pulled her into an alley. Bryce nodded to the other side of the street. We hustled across to a small church, pressed our backs against the brick wall, and inched closer to the alley.

"For the last time," Tracy said, "I didn't tell that Timberline kid anything. I said we didn't make it up."

"You swear?"

"Yes! I told you I'd stick with our story. You know I didn't want to tell those reporters anything, but you made me."

"You liked the attention as much as I did."

"Yeah, and now that guy is in jail."

"He'd be there anyway," Cammy said. "He's a drunk!"

Bryce and I ducked behind the concrete steps of the church as Tracy and Cammy walked toward the railroad tracks.

Bryce pulled out his recorder and smiled. "Maybe strike three was just a foul tip."

CHAPTER 74

◎ *Bryce* ◎

Ashley and I hurried to the police station, where I recognized the officer with the dog from the school sleepover. "Tell him," I said. "I'll bet he remembers you."

"Who did you lose this time?" the officer said, smiling.

"Can we talk to you about Danny?" Ashley said.

"It's not really my investigation. What do you want to know?"

"Is it true he confessed?" Ashley said.

The officer frowned. "I really can't talk about specifics. . . ."

I pulled out my recorder. "We think the girls are lying."

He dipped his head. "Really?"

I punched the Play button. The officer leaned close, and I turned up the volume. When the recording finished, he stood. "Stay right here."

A few minutes later he reappeared with the chief of police, who introduced himself and showed us into a room.

"Can we keep this?" the chief said.

I nodded.

The chief rubbed his cheek. "We've believed those girls from the start. Everything they said checked out. Even found some duct tape in that shed. Still had the price tag on it." He turned to the canine cop. "Officer Ormsby, go to the hardware store and have them go over the register receipts. See if anybody bought some tape about that time."

The chief thanked us and said he'd be in touch. Then he saw Ashley's candle catalog. "Dance studio?"

She nodded. "Bought anything yet?"

"There was this little thing I've been thinking about for the dining-room table."

Officer Ormsby stared at him.

The chief cleared his throat. "It's for my wife, Bill. Now didn't I give you an assignment?"

CHAPTER 75

❀ Ashley ❀

Mom and Sam were impressed. The phone rang after dinner and Sam answered. He put a hand over the mouthpiece. "They made a copy of your recording. We can go pick up the machine."

I was already looking for my shoes.

"Let's hurry," Sam said. "It's supposed to rain, and the wind is already picking up." As we headed to the car, he added, "You guys are getting good at this detective stuff. The chief said your information helped a lot."

Sam parked on the street across from the station, but before we could get out, Bryce grabbed Sam's shoulder. "Wait."

Cammy and Tracy were being led into the police station.

CHAPTER 76

Bryce

Neither Ashley nor I wanted to see Cammy and Tracy. Solving this puzzle was one thing. Taking responsibility for turning them in was another. We waited a few minutes, then walked into the police station behind Sam.

Officer Ormsby waved us into the waiting area and handed me the recorder. "We found a duct tape purchase at the hardware store on the afternoon of the attack. A cashier remembered two girls buying the tape that day."

"Where are they?" Ashley said.

"One is in the room at the end of the hall. The other is in that room." He nodded to the other end of the station house.

"Do they know what's going on?" Ashley said.

He shook his head and glanced at Sam. "Your kids are part of this investigation. Come with me."

CHAPTER 77

❀ Ashley ❀

Officer Ormsby led us into a small room with video monitors. On one screen we saw Tracy sitting at a table next to her father. Her hands were folded in her lap. On another screen, Cammy sat with her mother. They both looked like they needed a smoke. I felt sorry for them. They looked scared, and their parents looked grim.

The chief went into Tracy's room, plopped in a chair, and rubbed his face like he was exhausted. "Sorry to bring you down here tonight, but we have a development."

"He confessed?" Tracy's father said.

"No, he sure didn't," the chief said. "Still says he never touched your daughter." He looked at Tracy. "Anything you want to tell me?"

Tracy frowned and shook her head.

"Since we can't find much hard evidence linking him, we'd like you and your friend to take a polygraph. Know what that is?"

Tracy shook her head.

"A lie detector test?" her father said.

"Yeah. This guy is in big trouble, and we need the test as evidence."

It looked to me like Tracy's face turned pale. Her dad looked at her.

"I'll leave you alone for a minute," the chief said. "Think about it."

As soon as the chief was gone, Tracy's father said, "What's the matter?"

Tracy started crying.

The chief then visited Cammy and her mother, pulled out the recorder, and set it on the table.

"What's this, Officer?" Cammy's mom said.

The chief looked at Cammy. "You want to tell her, or do you want me to?"

"I don't know what you're talking about."

On the other video screen Tracy had put her head on the table and was sobbing.

"Cammy," the chief said, "we have an innocent man in our jail, don't we? Isn't it time you told us the truth?"

"You don't believe her?" Cammy's mom said.

The chief stared at Cammy. "This is your chance. Right here. Get it out in the open."

Cammy seemed to shrink into her chair, like the Wicked Witch of the West in *The Wizard of Oz*. "I told you the truth. Why don't you believe me?"

The chief pushed a button on the recorder, and Cammy's voice filled the room.

Cammy's mom turned to her, looking like she was about to explode.

Finally Cammy spoke. "Tracy and I were goofing off at school, and I knew you'd ground me for being late to babysit. When we went past the Toot Toot and saw that guy, we figured everybody would believe us. We bought the tape and tied each other up."

I looked at Bryce. He looked as sad as I felt. Sometimes the truth makes you feel bad and good at the same time.

CHAPTER 78

Bryce

The whole story came out in the news the next day. One TV station announced a series called "When Kids Lie."

The TV news also showed Danny walking out of jail with his mother and father. He had shaved and was smiling, his arm in a sling. The family waved off reporters as they drove away.

I wondered if Danny knew we were the ones who had helped get him released.

All anyone could talk about at school the next few days was Cammy and Tracy. A rumor said that one or both of them had run away, but we had learned not to believe everything we heard.

I couldn't stop thinking about Sam. He had been on the phone nonstop one night and in his office till late another. Mom seemed upset and hadn't worked much on her new book.

Leigh became almost a stranger. She stayed out—"studying," she said—and when she came home she just went to her room. She didn't ask Mom or Sam to let her drive and get her night hours in. The tension was about to kill me.

Who was Sam?

CHAPTER 79

❀ Ashley ❀

The fateful night came when we had to turn in our candle orders. I had only five on my sheet. I tried to get Mom to buy more, but she said Mrs. Gunderson at the dance studio would understand. She didn't know Mrs. Gunderson very well.

We handed our orders in at the beginning of the hour, and when the session was over, we all sat on the floor.

"You know that the person from each class who turns in the most orders gets a special prize," Mrs. Gunderson said. She held up the ballet shoes, and I knew this was the perfect Sunday school example of coveting. I wanted the shoes bad, but I had no chance.

"Well, the person with the most sales . . ."

Please don't drag this out.

". . . is Ashley Timberline."

It felt like I'd won an Academy Award without being nominated. I couldn't believe it. Surely many other girls had sold more than five candles.

Mrs. Gunderson held out the shoes and smiled. "Ashley sold 45 units."

Everybody clapped as I walked to the front. "But, Mrs. Gunderson," I whispered, "I didn't sell 45."

She showed me two order slips. The one on top had five measly signatures. The one on the bottom was filled with 40 items and only one signature.

Harriet Ingram's.

An envelope was taped to it. When everyone had gone, I opened it and pulled out a folded sheet.

> Dear Ashley,
>
> Officer Ormsby told us what you and your brother did. We can never thank you enough. Danny is doing better. He's at home now and says he wants to change. We're taking him for counseling next week.
>
> I'm so glad I got to meet you, and I hope these orders help.
>
> Love,
>
> Harriet

CHAPTER 80

Bryce

Jeff Alexander called after school and asked me to come to his house. "I have something to show you," he said.

I got there in record time. Jeff met me outside and waved me to the garage. He had a Boston Red Sox hat pulled low, and he seemed to have a spring in his step.

He opened the garage door slowly and I saw the tandem, blue with silver stripes. The backseat had a carrier behind it.

"A bike shop in the Springs donated it," Jeff said, beaming. "Want to try it?"

I hopped on the front, and Jeff climbed on the back. The driveway had gravel on it, so it was difficult getting to the street, but once we were there, we took off. Jeff didn't weigh much, and we flew down the hill whooping and hollering.

I looked back and saw Jeff pull off his hat and wave it in the air. "Wahoo! This is going to be the best summer ever!"

His bald head used to make me cringe, but now I barely noticed. Jeff was Jeff, hair or not.

I pulled over at a little park. Kids screamed as they ran through the playground equipment. Jeff and I found two open swings and sat.

"Can't believe I'm actually going to do this," he said.

"And I'm going to be there the whole way."

We talked about the supplies we would need and how much training we'd have to have before the race started.

"It's kind of like the Tour de France," Jeff said. "It'll be hard, but is there anything good in life that isn't hard?"

"Twinkies."

He laughed, then got quiet. "Ever had anything that stuck in your head that you couldn't get rid of? You know, something you couldn't figure out?"

Sam, I thought. "Sure. Why?"

"Why God lets bad stuff happen." He pulled his hat low over his eyes again. "I don't blame God anymore about this. I mean, I don't think he gave me cancer to punish me—I used to. I tried to think of all the things I'd done wrong and figure out which one made me get this." He pointed to his head. "But I'm never going to get married or have kids. I might not even get to graduate high school—I can tell the doctors even think eighth grade is a stretch."

"You're gonna beat this," I said. "The medicine they have, the treatment. You'll probably outlive all of us."

Jeff smiled. “I hope. But what if . . . what if we don’t even get to go on this ride?”

“We’re riding in the mountains this summer together. That’s it. End of story.”

Jeff smiled even bigger. “Yeah. We’re really going to do it, aren’t we, Bryce?”

CHAPTER 81

❀ Ashley ❀

Bryce and I agreed that we would tell only one person we could trust about the whole thing, and I chose Hayley. I didn't want word that we were responsible for uncovering Tracy and Cammy's lie getting back to them any more than I wanted to date Skeeter Messler.

Hayley promised she wouldn't tell anyone. "I hear they might be taken to the detention center. That place is as awful as jail. Maybe worse."

When I got home from dance class, Mom handed me a letter that had been stuck in the newspaper slot under our mailbox.

To: Ashley Timberline and her brother (I don't know his name.)
Fr: Danny Ingram

I know my mom wrote you, but I wanted to thank you personally for what you did to help me. I don't deserve how nice some people have been.

Maybe one day you and your brother can come to my parents' farm and ride horses or something. We have a three-legged dog that needs company.

Anyway, I'm leaving town for a treatment place to try and get my life together. Thanks again for believing me.

Sincerely,
Danny

CHAPTER 82

Bryce

I was thinking about my dad when Sam walked into my room. He sat on the bed.

"What?" I said.

He dug in his pocket and placed a letter on the bed. I stared at it like it was a dead fish.

"Ever seen this before?"

"Yes, sir," I said.

"Been snooping?"

"More like figuring."

"Figuring?"

"You told us you killed our father, and then you wouldn't say anything more. What was I supposed to do, let it go? I looked at some of your letters, yeah."

Sam nodded. "What did you find out?"

"I haven't pieced it all together, but I think you used to be in the military and maybe Marshall is a nickname."

"Go on," Sam said.

"Well, there's nobody in town who knows you longer than a few years. I can't find you in any military database. And the Social Security letter—"

"You opened my Social Security letter?" Sam said.

"It was open. It listed income for only the last four years. But you said you started working when you were a teenager. Why wouldn't it list income from years before?"

Sam had every right to be mad. He could tell Mom and lock me in my room until I turned 18. Instead he picked up the letter and carefully put it in his shirt pocket. "Come on. It's time we finish that talk I started a few weeks ago."

CHAPTER 83

❀ Ashley ❀

The scene felt familiar. All of us sat around the living room—except Dylan, who was in his room. Leigh had come out of hibernation and sat with her hair hiding her face. Sam paced in front of the fireplace.

The night had turned colder, and even though it was spring, a gentle snowfall covered the ground.

Sam rubbed his neck and took a breath. "I apologize for leaving you hanging. Part of me wanted to tell you everything, but I've been counseled that it was better not to. Now I know it's important you know the truth. Needless to say, you're going to have to keep this secret your whole lives."

He pulled out an envelope. "Bryce found this. I thought it was lost." He handed it to Leigh. "This is a birthday card I sent Leigh's mother before we were married. Most everything about my life before is gone, erased." He looked at Bryce. "I'm glad you found that."

Sam sat with his back to the fire. "My real name is Marshall Faulkner. My parents still live on a farm in West Virginia, but they don't know where I am, just that I'm alive. I fly over the farm every now and then and wish I could go back."

"Why can't you?" I said.

Sam looked at Mom, then continued. "I was in the army, a special antiterrorist tactical unit. They sent us all over the world. It wasn't a pleasant assignment, but all of us knew it had to be done.

"Many years ago, when Leigh was about Dylan's age, we caught up to a really nasty guy named Asim bin Asawe. He was responsible for bombings and the deaths of a lot of innocent American civilians, and he had a bunch of followers doing his dirty work. One night my team and I arrested or killed a couple dozen of his people.

"Asawe got away, and he let us know he'd have his revenge. Somehow he found out about me. Had my name because I was the leader of the team."

Leigh pulled the hair from her face and sat up, staring wide-eyed at her father.

"Years went by and I took a job in Washington for the defense department." He bit his lip. "Leigh's mom always wanted to go to England, had dreamed of visiting castles and walking the moors. So we planned a two-week vacation for the four of us. Everybody was excited. By then Leigh was almost 12 and Kayla was going into first grade.

"At the last minute, Leigh got a terrible ear infection. She couldn't fly until she got an antibiotic, so I told Lynn to go ahead with Kayla, and Leigh and I would catch up with them."

Sam stood and his chin quivered. "We dropped them off at the airport and went straight to the doctor's office. In the waiting room everybody was glued to the TV. A plane had gone down.

"We rushed home, listening to the reports, hoping, praying. And then the news came that it was Lynn and Kayla's plane. The next day the networks reported that Asim bin Asawe had claimed responsibility for the attack. He called it revenge against the American military."

Sam turned to Bryce and me. "That's why I said I killed your father. He was also on that plane, and the bomb that destroyed it was put there to kill me."

CHAPTER 84

Bryce

I wanted to hug Sam. I wanted to say something—anything—to make him feel better. I couldn't imagine how hard it had been to hold in that story so long.

"When they released the passenger list," Sam continued, "my name was on it. I got in touch with one of the antiterrorism directors, and he agreed we should let it stand. Leigh and I took on new identities."

I looked at Leigh. "What was your name?"

"Mary."

"That's why my Social Security card doesn't list income from way back," Sam said. "All the evidence of my previous life has been wiped away."

"Do you ever worry that this Asawe guy is going to find you?" Ashley said.

Sam nodded. "Remember when the newspaper wanted to interview you about the accident near Gold Town? I couldn't let them get a picture of us. Something like that could lead Asawe or his people right to our door."

I had seen all the terrible things terrorists had done in the past few years. They were so evil it was almost like they weren't human. I wondered if this was the reason Sam didn't believe in God.

"Your parents know you're okay?" Ashley said.

Sam nodded. "I couldn't let them believe I was dead. I've stayed away to protect them, but one day I'll go back."

The fire crackled and the wood smell wafted into the room. Pippin and Frodo curled up on the couch at Ashley's feet.

A voice broke the silence. "It wasn't your fault, Sam." It was Mom. I guess she already knew this story.

"You didn't kill anybody—those terrorists did," Ashley said.

Sam was near tears.

I wanted to say something too, but I was scared to talk.

CHAPTER 85

❀ Ashley ❀

Some say twins know what each other is thinking, that we can almost read each other's minds. I guess that sometimes happens with Bryce and me. But most of the time I have no idea what's going on in his brain. For instance, I never expected him to say what he said to Sam that night.

"Can I call you Dad?" Bryce said.

Sam looked at him. Then Bryce stood, and the two melted into a big hug.

"You bet," Sam said. "And I'm proud to call you my son." He glanced at me. "I'm proud of both of you."

Pretty soon all of us, Leigh included, were standing in the middle of the room, arms around each other. Pippin and Frodo jumped at my legs, trying to get in on the act. I don't know if our real dad or Sam's wife and other daughter could see us right then, but I hoped they could. And I hoped Sam and Leigh would believe in God someday.

We were all hugging when Mom gasped.

Dylan walked in wearing three pairs of socks, my dancing shoes, and a smile. "Wha's goin' on?" he said.

It felt good to laugh.

About the Authors

JERRY B. JENKINS (jerryjenkins.com) is the writer of the Left Behind series. He owns the Jerry B. Jenkins Christian Writers Guild, an organization dedicated to mentoring aspiring authors. Former vice president for publishing for the Moody Bible Institute of Chicago, he also served many years as editor of *Moody* magazine and is now Moody's writer-at-large.

His writing has appeared in publications as varied as *Reader's Digest, Parade, Guideposts,* in-flight magazines, and dozens of other periodicals. Jenkins's biographies include books with Billy Graham, Hank Aaron, Bill Gaither, Luis Palau, Walter Payton, Orel Hershiser, and Nolan Ryan, among many others. His books appear regularly on the *New York Times, USA Today, Wall Street Journal,* and *Publishers Weekly* best-seller lists.

Jerry is also the writer of the nationally syndicated sports story comic strip *Gil Thorp,* distributed to newspapers across the United States by Tribune Media Services.

Jerry and his wife, Dianna, live in Colorado and have three grown sons and three grandchildren.

CHRIS FABRY is a writer and broadcaster who lives in Colorado. He has written more than 40 books, including collaboration on the Left Behind: The Kids series.

You may have heard his voice on Focus on the Family, Moody Broadcasting, or Love Worth Finding. He has also written for Adventures in Odyssey and Radio Theatres.

Chris is a graduate of the W. Page Pitt School of Journalism at Marshall University in Huntington, West Virginia. He and his wife, Andrea, have been married 22 years and have nine children, two birds, two dogs, and one cat.

CONFIDENTIAL	Red Rock Mysteries.com
	The first 4 books now available:
	#1 Haunted Waters
	#2 Stolen Secrets
	#3 Missing Pieces
	#4 Wild Rescue
	WATCH FOR THE NEXT 4 BOOKS COMING SEPTEMBER 2005!

COOL
2
.com
READ